Anthony Price lives in Canterbury. An avid reader and film fanatic, and having always wanted to be a writer, he was first published at age fifteen. Since achieving his MA in Creative Writing he has had several short stories published in e-zines and anthologies, along with his first novel, *The House of Wood*, and his own horror anthology, *Tales of Merryville*, all of which available to buy on Amazon and at many book retailers.

Follow him at:
Website – http://anthonyprice84.wix.com/anthony-price-author
Facebook – https://www.facebook.com/anthonyjpricepage
Twitter – @anthonyprice84

Vigilante Chronicles: Book One

High Voltage

ANTHONY PRICE

Vigilante Chronicles: Book One

High Voltage

Vanguard Press

VANGUARD PAPERBACK

A CIP catalogue record for this title is
available from the British Library.

ISBN 978 178465 041 4

Vanguard Press is an imprint of
Pegasus Elliot MacKenzie Publishers Ltd.
www.pegasuspublishers.com

First Published in 2015

Vanguard Press
Sheraton House Castle Park
Cambridge England

Printed & Bound in Great Britain

This is for all those facing adversity
that never stop
fighting.

Acknowledgements

Firstly, I'd like to thank the editors and staff at Pegasus Publishers for not only believing in me as a writer, but for having as much faith in this book as I do.

A big thank you has to go to my sister, Stacey, who pushed me to not give up on this one. Your opinion I'll always seek out first when it comes to editing.

But the biggest thank you will always go to my parents, who raised me to think big and to never let any obstacle stand in my way. Without your love, I wouldn't be around today.

Finally, thank you to everyone who buys this book. Your continued and dedicated support means the world. Without you, I wouldn't have a job.

Chapter One

Darkness crept over the city like a velvet blanket. The silent moon hung above the metropolis, bathing it in a milky glow, as the population began to bed down for the night. The entertainment district was buzzing as usual. The neon glow from the many electric billboards stood out vibrantly against the quieter areas of the city, which like the sky, had dropped into darkness.

The streets were deserted outside the Zygonia City Museum. The museum itself stood in stark contrast to the modern buildings around it. It was one of the oldest structures in the city. Originally, it had been the headquarters of the local government. The people of the city had fought tooth and nail to save it from modern developers who wanted to bring it 'in line' with its surroundings. Hearing of the citizens' plight, a wealthy philanthropist had purchased the building and turned into one of the most famous museums in the world. It housed some of the rarest artefacts known to man and was currently home to a recent discovery, which was believed by some to have originated from another planet. It was known as the Raman Staff. However, after discovering the staff, scientists had carried out tests, which suggested that the artefact was nothing more than that – a piece of history with no evidence to support its extraterrestrial origins or its ability to grant the owner unimaginable power. But not everyone was convinced.

In a dark alley adjacent to the museum, a lone van sat parked discreetly out of view of any prying eyes. To anybody looking, all that could be seen was a solitary occupant, who appeared to be listening to the radio. The sound of the soccer game emanated from the van and penetrated the deep silence. The figure seemed to be enthralled. He let out a sudden cheer as it was announced that the Zygonia Zappers had won 3-0 against the Redrock Chiefs. As his elation subsided, he reached over and switched it off. It was almost time.

He leant over to the glove compartment and took out a small, semi-automatic pistol – a Walther P99. All he had to do was sit and wait for the man who had hired him.

Jacob looked at his watch for the tenth time in less than an hour. Not long now. He was determined that this would be his last job; after this he was going straight. The man who had hired him had promised to pay more than he could ever dream of. But Jacob felt uneasy. He'd never broken into a museum before and now he was breaking in to the world's most prestigious one. It was a step up from bank jobs. He didn't even know what it was that he was stealing, but he knew it must be worth a fortune; a fortune that could be his if he played his cards right. He planned on getting inside the museum and stealing whatever it was he was supposed to steal and then disappearing with it. Maybe it would be something he could sell on the black market? He could make millions, much more than this mysterious benefactor had offered, despite it being a substantial sum. He and his family could finally get out of the slums and live a life he had always dreamt of, but one that had always been beyond his reach.

As he sat pondering a bright future, two headlights pierced through the darkness coming towards him very slowly from the opposite direction. He looked down at his watch. It was time.

He turned in his seat to look through the small hatch that was located over his left shoulder. He opened it and peered through to the back of the van. Three rough-looking men huddled together with various pieces of equipment and weaponry, looked back at him.

"Yo, boys, time to kit up!" he announced in his gruff voice.

The men in the back all hurriedly obeyed his order. They were all professional criminals who had been on jobs with Jacob before. He trusted them with his life. Shame I have to double cross them too, he thought, as a black BMW parked itself in front of the van, its headlights glaring at him. Jacob couldn't tell how many people were in the car, but a single tall male stepped out of the driver's door. It appeared that he was alone, but it was certainly the man who had hired him; Jacob would never forget that face.

The man's features were hideously disfigured by a single scar which ran in a diagonal line across his face. He wore a black eye-patch over his left eye and the right side of his jaw drooped where a sharp implement had possibly been used in an attempt to kill him. His one good eye had a look of pure evil. His groomed silver hair contrasted against his uneven features. This was not a man Jacob wanted to confront openly. However, Jacob was the professional thief and this man obviously didn't know the first thing about breaking in to a place unannounced or he wouldn't have hired him. And there, Jacob thought to himself, was where his success would be. He would break into the museum, locate the required item and steal anything else of value. Then he and his boys could overwhelm their client by sheer force of numbers. It was a foolproof plan.

He had begun to sweat and his mouth was dry. He sipped at a bottle of water. For some reason he still couldn't shift his uneasy feeling that had been building all evening. I just wish I knew more about this guy, he thought. All he could remember was the night he had been hired.

**

It had been a night much like this one. As usual, Jacob had gone down to the local dive bar to escape his relentless, nagging wife. He planned on getting stone-cold drunk whilst watching the Zappers get through to the semi-finals of the National Cup. He had been deep into his third pint when One-Eye, as Jacob named him then, had approached.

"Are you Jacob Zlovski?" the man asked flatly.

"Yeah, what's it to you?" The words had been so slurred that they were almost incomprehensible. Jacob took another swig of beer as his new companion sat down opposite. He tried to ignore him, but One-Eye just stared, making Jacob feel uncomfortable. He hated it when people stared, especially when they were uninvited.

"You got a problem?"

"I have a proposition for you. I work for a very influential man who requires your particular skills. We hear you're the best." One-Eye's deep velvety voice was alluring. But Jacob wasn't interested in finding work and the look of the guy gave him the creeps.

"Not interested, friend. Now get lost!" Jacob tried to sound tough and disinterested, but to his dismay he could hear a faint strain in his voice that matched his growing nervousness. It was obvious his companion had noticed it too.

One-Eye sat back in his chair; a faint smile began to appear at the corners of his mouth. It gave him an even more menacing look.

"My boss is prepared to pay whatever it takes to complete the job." One-Eye's voice was like a cat purring; so soft and gentle. Jacob could feel himself hanging on every word. His mind was drifting with each passing syllable. It's just the alcohol, he hoped. He shook his head to clear it.

"Look, I'm sorry. I don't do bank jobs any more. If you don't mind I'd like to be alone."

One-Eye still didn't budge. Jacob took another sip of his pint and stared intently at the TV screen. He hoped if he ignored him long enough, One-Eye would get up and go. It wasn't working. Who is this creep? Jacob wondered. For all he knew, this stranger could be a cop. And he hated those. Jacob could feel the man's single eye boring in to his skull, the same deadly smile on his lips. He could be insane!

"This is no bank job. But if you aren't interested I will inform my employer. He's a man who insists on getting bad news immediately."

One-Eye rose from his seat and started to edge away. Jacob's heart had begun to race. Not a bank job. Then what job was it? It could be big. His curiosity got the better of him.

"Wait!" he shouted. One-Eye turned back to face him. "Who do you work for?" Jacob asked.

"I can't divulge that kind of information. Let's just say, he's a man of immense power and influence. One that could change your life for the better," One-Eye added sarcastically.

Jacob's interest piqued. There were only a handful of people in Zygonia he could think of that met that description; there was one guy that supposedly killed off all the other people with the same name if they didn't agree to change it. But that was just an urban myth. The guy's bank balance, however, wasn't. It had to be him.

"What would one of the richest men in the world want with me?" Jacob asked. "He could hire anyone."

"Let's just say he's heard of your impressive leadership skills," One-Eye replied, his voice alluring.

This job could change his life. One-Eye continued to stare at him, never once taking his eye away.

Jacob had an overwhelming need to know more about the job, even though deep down it was a bad mistake.

"Please sit down, tell me more." He motioned to the chair One-Eye had just vacated.

"Maybe we could move to somewhere more private." One-Eye said. It was more a statement than a question.

Jacob led his mysterious guest to a secluded booth at the rear of the bar. He could sense that he was making a huge mistake but he just couldn't stop. He was compelled. The two men sat.

"My boss needs you to help him acquire an artefact from the National Museum. He's heard of your unique talents when it comes to security systems."

"What artefact?" Jacob asked. Best to get straight to the point.

"That information won't be necessary. My boss will provide any equipment you need. Your payment is six-hundred-thousand US dollars."

Wow, six-hundred-thousand! That was a huge sum of money, Jacob mused. More than he could even imagine. It didn't sound too difficult, but it did sound too good to be true.

"Do I get to pick my own team?"

"If you wish. Do we have an agreement?"

One-Eye's single eye grew wide as he reached out to shake Jacob's hand. Jacob felt helpless. The hypnotic allure of the man was just too much.

The men shook hands.

"Good. Be at this location. The date and time is also listed." He passed Jacob a folded piece of yellow paper and turned to leave.

"Wait! What do I call you?"

One-Eye stopped with his back to Jacob. A deadly glint appeared in his eye.

"Call me... Pulse!"

Yeah, okay. Night, One–Eye, Jacob thought.

***

Jacob's reverie was brought to an abrupt halt as Pulse tapped on the van window. Jacob unwound it.

"Are your men ready?" Pulse asked.

"Yes, sir."

"Drive your van to the service entrance at the back of the museum and wait for me there."

Jacob pressed the button to wind the window back up and started the engine as Pulse crept off in to the night. Yes, sir, no, sir, three bags full, sir! This guy was beginning to grate on Jacob's last nerve.

"That guy's creepy." Tad, the youngest in the crew at eighteen, exclaimed as he checked the barrel of his pistol. "Why do we need these anyway?"

"Just shut it and let me deal with him," Jacob snapped back.

He was beginning to wonder if six-hundred-thousand dollars was worth all the hassle. But with the debt his wife had racked up he knew he had no choice. And it wasn't just debt. He had two young kids to support. He never wanted them having to follow his footsteps in to crime. With that kind of money he could set them up in college. They would be set for life. That was the real reason he had agreed to this in the first place. His kids were the only reason he would *ever* screw over his friends.

Jacob pulled into the back entrance of the museum. He saw Pulse standing there, waiting for them, with the entrance already open. How'd he get here? He is one creepy dude, Jacob thought, but he didn't dare voice his opinion to the boys. He could see they were jumpy enough.

As the van ground to a halt, the men jumped out and circled Jacob. He explained the plan to them and then informed Pulse they were ready. Dark clouds had formed, half covering the gleaming moon, as the group stepped in to the museum.

Chapter Two

The dimly lit corridors of the museum gave the entire place a nightmarish feel. Ghostly faces of waxwork models beckoned from the darkness, their features locked in a timeless expression. A small sliver of light shone through the only window in the corridor. Museums look completely different at night than they do during the day, Jacob thought, as he and his crew followed Pulse down the long hallway towards the stairs. Apparently, their target was the new Egyptian display located in the lower west wing of the museum. He still had no idea which artefacts they were stealing, but he really didn't care, as long as it would fetch a huge sum on the black market.

As they rounded the corner and reached the top of the stairs, Pulse informed them that the night guards had been dealt with. Dealt with? Jesus. Did he mean dead? Jacob wondered.

He looked over his right shoulder to see his men behind him. Each one was blindly following, but he could deduce from looking into their eyes that they had come to the same conclusions. Something just didn't feel right. Jacob couldn't put his finger on it; it was as if he was wading through a murky swamp that was determined to drag him under. Part of him wanted to turn and run, but the other half felt compelled to complete the job for his kids. The guys may have been a bunch of thieves, but they weren't killers. Their leader, however, obviously didn't mind getting his hands dirty. As the group made their way down the giant staircase in the main entrance, Jacob found his fears very well grounded. There was an audible gasp from his crew.

Three security guards lay dead on the floor. Bullet holes in their skulls leaked a sticky red liquid. It had splattered all over the security station. Puddles had begun to form around the bodies, giving them a horrifying outline, which stood out against the brilliant white floor tiles.

"Jesus," exclaimed Knox, a huge bull of a man. He was Jacob's muscle and by the look of things he was going to be needed, especially if they were to get one over on the freak. And that's exactly what Pulse was – a freak who was prepared to kill.

"What the hell happened?" The question was aimed at Pulse.

"They felt compelled to commit suicide. So very tragic. I'm sure they will be missed. Now wait here, I'll be back."

Pulse strolled off in the direction of the west wing. The thieves were left standing in horror. Each man looked from one to the other as they huddled around the security station not knowing what to do.

"I don't like this, boss," said Tad, who by now had turned a pasty white. "He ain't right in the head, that one."

"Yeah let's git outta 'ere whiles our heads don't leak like theirs do," said Smithy, in his usual nasal, snivelling tone.

They had a point. Jacob knew he should call the whole deal off, but he was so close to a dream life. He took a look around. The museum was full of rare and exotic items that collectors would pay a pretty penny for. He had to calm the men's fears. Nothing was going to get in his way. "It's all right boys. I got a plan, see. We're gonna be rich."

"Oh yeah, what plan?" asked Knox.

Their faces lit up like a Christmas tree at the mention of becoming rich. Jacob had no intention of cutting them in. But at the moment he needed them to help overwhelm Pulse. Strength in numbers, he thought. So he burst headlong into the explanation of his plan.

***

Pulse stalked through the myriad corridors like a shadow; smooth and agile. His first port of call was the CCTV control room. Then he would return to the security station. It had to look like he was never here. A false recording on the security hard drive and careful editing should do the trick, he thought. He was glad to be on his own; he worked better that way. And anything had to be better than being with those inbred cretins. He couldn't be gone long though or they would get suspicious. Not that he cared if they did. His employer on the other hand would be furious if anything went wrong. And that Jacob was certainly no fool. His expertise in problem solving and getting his team to carry out their tasks would be needed to break through the state of the art security system that had been shipped in to guard the item they were after. The Raman Staff; a weapon that could be the most powerful ever to be discovered. The thought made him tingle with excitement as he went about his task.

He was halfway through the editing on his palm-top, which he had wired into the CCTV, when he noticed his reflection in the security monitor screen. The long, jagged scar, which disfigured his features, brought back painful memories. His special ops team that was massacred during a failed mission in the Congo. The torture and depravation he went through at the behest of his captors all came flooding back. It was then that he had discovered his unique skills. Had it not been for this new discovery, he never would have escaped and found the man who took him in. He owed that man his life, but his son was different – some would say unhinged. But Pulse had promised to watch over him, so that's what he would do, no matter what.

He quickly finished destroying any evidence that could connect him to the crime. A good job, he thought, as he calmly made his way back down the corridor.

He took a quick look at the Egyptian display. There was the staff, illuminated under gold lights in the middle of the cavernous room – a room, which was shut off by a thick wall of bulletproof glass. It was also locked by an electronic data pad. No wonder they only employed three night watchmen, he realised. The room was virtually impregnable. Even if they did get in, they had to shut off the laser alarm system and crack open the casing surrounding the staff. It was near enough impossible. He just hoped Jacob would live up to his reputation.

***

By the time Pulse returned, Jacob had finished filling in his crew on the plan. They would wait until they had the item and anything else of value they could carry. Then they would overpower Pulse and scarper. They would be rich! What they didn't know was Jacob could seal them all in and get away by himself. By the time anyone found them he would be in Cuba. To the police it would just look like a botched heist; it would be ages before they even believed the remaining men that he was here. Perfect!

"I've located the Egyptian exhibition," Pulse informed the group as he walked towards them.

He could sense they were edgy. They had no doubt been planning to double-cross him. Oh well. He didn't want to spoil his fun by indicating to them that he was aware of their plan, so he continued.

"The item we require is a staff. It's held in a room with a laser alarm system and a three-foot-thick sheet of bulletproof glass. The item itself is in a case made of similar material. Any questions?"

The four men sat staring at him, bemusement written all over their faces.

Pulse smiled. "No? Then follow me please, gentlemen."

Each of them grudgingly obeyed. All this for a damn staff, Jacob reasoned. There must be something else in the room of value; no one would go to that much trouble for a lump of wood. Jacob thought he remembered something. He turned to Tad.

"Hey, Tad," he whispered. "Wasn't this place in the news last week?"

"Yeah, there was something about some stick from Egypt. Mom showed me the article."

That was it. Jacob remembered now. The stick, as Tad called it, was known as The Raman Staff. It was supposed to have mystical powers or something. This was turning into what promised to be a lucrative night.

They rounded a corner to be confronted by the glass barrier. Jacob walked over to the data pad, situated on the left. He stood there for a few seconds scratching his stubbly chin. This shouldn't be a problem. It would take Tad two minutes to attach the decoder and another thirty seconds to unlock the barrier, which would then open automatically. State of the art, my ass, Jacob joked to himself.

"Tad, you're up first. Watch us experts at work, Mr Pulse. This won't take long."

Tad obliged and within minutes the barrier was opening. He let out a whoop of delight at his success. Tad was a genius when it came to technology. The deep vibrations of the mechanism reverberated down the dark hall. Pulse stood watching, his muscular arms folded across his chest. Impressive, he thought, as Jacob stepped forward to the entrance way.

"Good job, Tad. Smithy, you reckon you can divert these beams?" Jacob asked.

"Ain't seen lazy beams like these 'uns before. I reckon it'll take me twenty minutes ta do a proper job," Smithy replied in his broken English.

"Good. You got ten minutes."

The man wasn't the sharpest tool in the box when it came to books and general knowledge, but as a thief he was one of the best. Jacob had never come across an alarm system that could beat Smithy.

He went about his task while Jacob daydreamed about his future. I think I'll get a yacht. I've always wanted to go sailing. He smiled and swivelled his head to look around. Pulse was staring straight at him. Jacob could swear he was grinning. It was hard to tell with his scar. Still, it made Jacob uneasy enough to stare at the floor until Smithy had managed to clear a safe path through the beams.

"'Ere boss, I dun it. It were 'ard work, but I dun it." Smithy spat out a wad of phlegm; his gums were missing several teeth, which was clear as he smiled.

In the centre of the room sat the staff. It was gold with gems encrusted down its length. One end was a hook, which appeared to be made of highly polished bone. Jacob and his men stood in awe around the thick glass case. This has to be the staff from the news, Jacob realised. Now all that stood in the way was a simple glass case; a few small explosive charges to crack the glass and the staff would be his.

"Knox, use four small charges. Nothing big. We don't want to disturb anything that could disrupt the beams."

"No problem, boss." Knox replied.

He was ex-military and a man of few words. Jacob was hoping the sheer size of the brute would be enough to dissuade Pulse from fighting back.

He took a sly look over his shoulder. Pulse was standing nonchalantly outside the huge room. Why is he just standing there? Jacob wondered. It was as if he was waiting for something other than the staff.

"Okay, everyone move unless you want glass in ya face," Knox said, with a rare grin.

The men moved back behind the wall near the entranceway. Knox pushed a small detonator in his hand.

Beep... bang!

The glass casing shattered, sprinkling razor sharp edges over the floor, which crunched under the men's boots as they rushed back over to the staff. There it was. Free. The four thieves had their backs to Pulse. They all smiled. The staff was beautiful up close. And it's all mine, Jacob thought, as he reached out to grasp it. He waited until it was firmly secured in his palm.

"Now!"

The four men spun to confront their client, weapons drawn. Four guns were pointing straight at Pulse.

"We'll be taking this," sneered Jacob. His crew gave a derogatory snort of laughter. Smithy was giggling like a school girl.

Pulse just smiled back. "Oh really?"

Suddenly, he threw his hands forward. Tad and Smithy were slung backwards into the rear wall. They had been struck by some sort of pulse. Smithy's head cracked against the wall. His lifeless body slumped to the ground, breaking one of the security beams. Alarms blared through the museum. Pulse's insane laughter could still be heard over the ringing. Jacob and Knox stood dumbfounded.

"I'll take those too!" With a twitch of Pulse's hand, the guns flew into the air. The two men left standing were paralysed with fear. Knox's gun turned in mid-air, held by invisible hands. The concentration on Pulse's face was intense. Small beads of sweat trickled down his forehead. He flicked his hand.

Bang!

Knox dropped like a stone with a single bullet in his brain. It was then that Jacob wet his pants. A grown man and he peed himself. He fell to his knees sobbing. It was supposed to be a foolproof plan.

Pulse stood over him. "I think that stick belongs to me."

The last thing Jacob heard was the alarm ringing, a click, then...

Bang!

***

Outside, the moon had finally slipped behind dense grey clouds that looked like giant winged creatures of doom. The BMW that had arrived just over an hour ago was still parked in the same spot. Only a handful of people had walked down the secluded street in that time. No one had paid any attention. There was nothing unusual about a parked car.

A solitary figure emerged out of the shadows. His silver hair gave him a wolfish look, his long, black coat swayed gently in the breeze. It would rain soon, he thought.

Pulse stalked towards the car with the staff in a leather case slung over his shoulder. As he approached, the rear window opened halfway. The sweet scent of a cigar wafted into the night air.

"Have you secured the item?"

"Yes, sir." Pulse hated calling this little upstart 'sir', but he had no choice. Remember your promise, he reminded himself.

"Good." The man was virtually purring with satisfaction. His deep, seductive voice was hypnotizing. "Have it sent to the R & D facility being set up. Dr Omar should be expecting you."

"Yes, sir."

The window wound back up and the driver started the engine. As the car began to pull away, the man puffed on his cigar. Perfect. Soon he would be more powerful than his father could've ever dreamt of. The old fool was too narrow-minded. But now his name would be synonymous with world conquest. Perfect.

Chapter Three

Sunlight beamed down through the classroom window. Out of the small number of students in the class, most were listening to Professor Drake in awe. He was giving his annual lesson on optics and electromagnetism and was attempting to explain Maxwell's equations on how light can be seen as an electromagnetic wave. But not all the students were paying attention.

Kellen Amos, one of the most gifted students in the class, sat with his head resting in his hand. He had done Maxwell's equations time and time again. It was simple stuff. The students in the class only had to look out of the window at the brilliant sunshine to understand what the professor was droning on about. Kellen was more intent at staring at the girl situated two rows in front of him.

Linzi Rollingson was one of the most beautiful girls he had ever seen. All through the first year of high school, Kellen was dying to ask her out on a date. Trouble was, he was just too shy. Not only was the girl beautiful, but she was also über intelligent. Her father was one of the world's greatest physicists. In fact, he was one of Kellen's all-time heroes, his inspiration for taking up physics in the first place. What would a girl like that see in me? he wondered. He was hopelessly in love but with no way of showing the girl his true feelings. As far as she knew, he was just another dorky school boy; an insignificant acquaintance. Anyway, rumour had it she was dating some lacrosse jock in his final year of college studying forensics. Casper Jackson, or Jasper Cackson. Kellen couldn't remember which. All he knew was that it was another damn jock stealing all the best girls. And not just any girl, one five years his junior. Why couldn't he get a girl his own age?

Kellen sighed. Bad move. Professor Drake had spotted him.

"Ahh, Mr Amos, my young prodigy. Maybe you can solve the equation?" His stuffy British accent got on most people's nerves, but Kellen thought it was pretty cool. He sounded like 007.

Kellen did hate being put on the spot though; his brain never wanted to work when called upon out of the blue. He could do this. "Umm… Uh…" He couldn't even work out a simple equation. That'll teach me for not listening, he thought.

His brain whirled furiously, trying to work it out. All eyes were on him. Got it! He was about to give the answer when the bell above his head gave out a shrill ringing, which hummed in his ears.

"Okay, class, read chapter eighteen and nineteen by the next session and complete the tasks." Professor Drake may well have been talking to empty seats. None of the students were listening. The murmur of multiple conversations on weekend plans was growing to a crescendo. "And I do mean *all* the tasks!" he added, having to shout to be heard over the din.

Kellen rushed to stuff his giant textbooks into his bag as quickly as he could. He wanted to get out of the classroom before being cornered by the professor.

After the last book was in his pack, he slung it over his shoulder. Damn, these books are heavy, he realised, as he walked towards the door trying his hardest to blend in. Ten steps… Six steps… Two steps left to go…

"Kellen, may I have a word please?"

Damn, too late. He was so close.

Professor Drake sat reading a document while Kellen shuffled his way over to the desk. The professor made him stand there for a few moments before putting down the folder. He looked at him sternly in the face. "Your grades are dropping, you're distracted in class. You can't even work out simple equations to which you already know the answers. Is everything okay?"

Despite his stern tone, Kellen could hear the note of sincerity in his voice. Professor Drake had been watching out for Kellen since he arrived at the Zygonia School of Excellence. He didn't want to worry him without cause.

"Everything's fine, Professor. I'm just tired, that's all. Nothing to worry about." Kellen smiled, but he could see the professor wasn't convinced.

A wry smile crept across the professor's lips. "This wouldn't have anything to do with Miss Rollingson?" he asked.

"No!" Kellen's face had gone bright red like a strawberry. He wanted the ground to open up and swallow him. How does he know?

"There's no need to get embarrassed. She is a very lovely girl." The professor's smile disappeared. "However, you can't let your feelings stand in the way of your work. You are a talented young scientist with tremendous potential. You need to start knuckling down and deal with your love life outside of my class, or you risk losing your scholarship. You have to pass this class to continue qualifying. Is that understood?"

The last thing Kellen wanted was to lose his scholarship. When the school administration board had offered him the place for excellence in physics, he'd jumped at the chance to move to the big city. Home wasn't exactly a happy place. Going back wasn't an option.

"Yes, Professor. I understand and I'm sorry. I won't get distracted again, I promise." He just hoped it was a promise he could keep.

"Good. In that case you can follow me." The professor's smile was back, although Kellen had no idea why.

"Where are we going?" he asked.

"You'll see, my boy. I'm sure you'll like it a lot. Follow me, please."

***

"Welcome to the lab," Professor Drake announced.
It was a huge, empty room except for the science equipment that could be seen scattered at various workstations. There was a constant buzzing of machinery.

"Now you've seen the smaller labs, but they are nothing compared to this one. This lab was funded by JonasTech and is used for research and development carried out by the staff here, including myself and JonasTech employees on occasion. What I want you to do is carry out an experiment concerned with advanced wave propagation with electromagnetism. Over here."

The professor beckoned him over to one of the bigger stations.

Great, Kellen mused. He wasn't relishing the thought of being stuck in a hot, stuffy lab all weekend. In fact, he could think of nothing worse. He had only just finished his own experiments in one of the smaller labs. Maybe the professor was testing him? he wondered. Experiments like these required a huge amount of concentration.

"Do you think you can handle that? It's a very simple procedure."

"Yeah, no problem. I won't let you down, Professor Drake," Kellen said with sincerity, although he wasn't convinced himself. All he had done lately was screw things up.

"Good lad. I knew you would be up to the challenge. Now don't forget, concentration is the key to success in science. I want you to record all your findings on my laptop and save it. You can have the results on my desk first thing Monday morning. Make sure if you leave, you switch off all of the equipment and put away any chemicals. We don't want any accidents now, do we?" He laughed and gave him a playful pat on the back. Then he left Kellen alone in the lab, closing the sealed doors behind him.

Kellen let out a huge sigh for the second time that day, as he looked out of the window at the beautiful sunshine. Last night had poured hard with rain, but you wouldn't know it if you saw the weather now. Birds were swooping among the trees singing their gleeful song. Groups of students were either sunbathing or playing sports on the green in the quad. One group was fooling around playing lacrosse.

And there she was; Linzi.

One of those guys must be her boyfriend, Kellen mused. He hadn't met him before, but he already disliked him. What was he doing on school grounds anyway? Just because he was a local sports star that doesn't mean he should be allowed to go wherever he wants, Kellen fumed. He could be a murderer, or a mugger. Anything.

He stepped away from the window. It wouldn't matter if he hadn't managed to get himself put in the lab; out there he still wouldn't be able to talk to her. If only he could think of something. They lived different lives. She was the popular daughter of a famous physicist and he was a shy, awkward nobody.

He slipped on his bright-white jacket and started to prepare the equipment needed for the experiment. He had done a similar one before, but nothing this large, or important. It looked complicated. Professor Drake's words reverberated around his brain. Concentration is the key to success in science. We'll soon find out, he thought. He would start with solids first. Time to corrupt some atomic structures.

He switched on the machine and sat down in front of the laptop to record his findings.

***

Two hours had passed. He had tested the effects of electromagnetic waves on various different materials. Now he had attached the electrical current to a tube of weird-looking green liquid. He switched the machine on. A surprise visitor walked in.

A short, slightly chubby guy came crashing through the doorway, munching on a doughnut. He had a look of sheer annoyance on his face. It was Dan Halladay, Kellen's best friend. They'd been friends since Kellen had joined the school. Both the target of the school bully's ridicule, the two of them had made a pact to stick together through thick and thin. Dan, despite his obsession with video games and comic books, couldn't really be classed as a geek per se, but he certainly had geeky qualities. He took another bite of his doughnut before speaking. "I've been searching for you everywhere!" he exclaimed, spraying crumbs all over the floor.

"Well, here I am."

The liquid had begun to bubble. He suddenly looked up, puzzled.

"How did you get in here?" Kellen asked, ignoring his friend's dismay. "There's a campus security guard and the door is electronically sealed. You have to enter the code on the data pad."

Dan looked back at him with feigned shock then laughed. "Dude, the security guy's asleep in his office and I'm a Computer Science whizz. A guy named Tad in the senior class showed me how to hack those new data pads. It's actually quite simple considering they are, and I quote, 'supposedly impossible to hack'." He let out a small childlike chuckle.

Kellen refocused his attention on the tube of liquid. But as he did so, Dan hopped up on to the work surface. Some of the liquid splashed on to Kellen's skin.

"Hey, watch it!" he shouted, rushing over to the tap.

"Oops. Sorry, dude," Dan apologised. "It's not toxic is it?"

"No, I don't think so," Kellen replied, checking first his hands and then the container. "It should be fine. Just be careful!"

"I'll try," Dan said, jumping off the work bench. "It's okay, I know CPR."

They both laughed, as Dan ran over and mimed restarting Kellen's heart, trying to give him mouth-to-mouth resuscitation. Kellen had forgotten all about the running experiment.

"What did you want me for anyway?"

"Ah, well. It's about these..." Dan pulled two tickets out of his back pocket. "Not one, but two tickets to the Tenth Annual Science Banquet."

"How the hell did you get those? They're like gold-dust. It's the first time that the school has been invited."

Dan may have been a big clown at heart, but he was a genius when it came to procuring certain items.

"Everyone will be there. It's being hosted by JonasTech..."

"...And Dr Rollingson is guest speaker," Dan finished, with a sly smirk. "Which gives you a chance to talk to Linzi, outside of this place. Am I brilliant or what?"

"You're a damn genius!"

Kellen's heart was racing as he took the ticket from Dan's hand. The banquet would give him and Linzi some common ground. And he could meet his hero, Dr Rollingson. This was going to be an awesome night, he thought, looking at the ticket.

Beaumont Park Hall. Start time, 8.30p.m.

He looked at his watch.

"Crap! We better get back to the dorm. It starts at eight thirty and it's six now. The bus'll be leaving school around seven thirty. We've got to change *and* get across town. We'll never make it."

"Calm down. There's plenty of time." Dan made Kellen wait while he finished his doughnut. "Now we can go."

The two boys jostled each other all the way out of the lab, sealing the door shut behind them. Their laughter could be heard across the quad. The bright sun was beginning to set beyond the horizon.

Kellen's experiment sat stranded on the work surface still running.

He had abandoned it.

And the liquid was bubbling out of control.

Chapter Four

The traffic in Zygonia City on a Friday night was horrendous. The masses that had been working hard all week used it as an excuse to blow off steam and go crazy. Throngs of party people lined the pavements, streaming past the cab window. Beaumont Park was all the way across town and at this rate they were never going to make it in time.

Kellen sat staring out of the glazed cab window with his mind all over the place. He wasn't happy that they had missed the school bus. He hated public transport with a passion, but he desperately wanted to make it to the banquet. The worst thing was, it was yet another thing he was going to get it in the neck for. He really was turning into one big screw-up. He was just glad that nothing else could go wrong.

Thoughts of Linzi seemed to be the predominate theme that threaded through his mind. He'd forgotten about Dan, who at that point was dozing in his seat next to him. He gave him a quick nudge in the ribs.

"Wake up!"

"But I'm sleepy and this is so boring. Why is it taking so long?" Dan whined.

"You're like a big kid." He leant forward. "Excuse me, sir. Is there a quicker way to Beaumont Park? We're kind of in a hurry."

"Yo, Jack, sit back, relax. Let me deal with the navigational issues. Louie's cabs never fail to get a customer to their destination on time. Damn kids, always gotta rush." The last part was more to himself than to his two passengers, but Kellen did as he was told.

"Jesus, it's stifling in here, or is it me?" Kellen asked.

"It's you," Dan replied, dozing back off to sleep.

Kellen was soaking with sweat. It didn't help that he had a thick, polyester tuxedo on. He had never liked dressing up. And he hated the damn bow-tie. He reached up to his throat to loosen it. He wasn't sure though if it was the tux mixed with the heat or his nerves making him feel so hot. He'd never felt so nervous in his life. All this for a woman, he thought, as he went back to staring out the window. Why is there so much traffic? As if he had psychically heard Kellen's thoughts, the taxi driver chimed up.

"Hey, you boys hear about that robbery at the National Museum last night?" he asked, watching them in his rear view mirror. They both looked at one another, but neither answered. The driver continued. "Yeah, the cops're all over it. Diverted all traffic aways from the place. What's a cabbie to do, huh? Butta-bing, butta-boom. I have to take less fares, y'know."

He stopped as he turned the taxi on to 85th Street. Just a few more blocks to go. Kellen took a look at his watch. 20.15.

The cabbie noticed. "Don't worry, son. I'll get yous dere."

Dan elbowed Kellen. "Hey, Kellen. What do you reckon they stole?"

"Ouch! Do you mind?" Kellen rubbed his ribs. "I don't know. Artefacts, maybe?" He really didn't care much. He just wanted this cab ride to end before Dan and the driver sent him insane.

"Actually, it was some kinda staff. It was only supposed to be here for a month," the cabbie added.

He and Dan then sat chatting about it for the next ten minutes. Suddenly, Beaumont Park came in to view.

"Here ya go, boys. That'll be thirty-two fifty. Don't skimp on the tip," he suggested, as he pulled up outside the huge hall.

Kellen handed over the fare. He stepped out of the cab, took a deep breath and waited for Dan. They watched the yellow cab pull off. Thank God that's over, Kellen thought, as Dan placed a hand on his shoulder.

"You ready to party?" he asked.

Kellen wasn't sure. His emotions were too mixed. It was making him feel nauseous. He was excited to hear Dr Rollingson speak, but he was nervous about seeing Linzi. How would he approach her? What would he say? He had to do it sometime or he would regret it forever. No time like the present. Time to be a man, Kellen, he thought. He turned to look at Dan and smiled. "Let's go."

Dan let out a hearty cheer as the pair climbed the mountain of marble stairs leading to the entrance.

Everybody seemed to be in high spirits for the evening. Dan advised that they shouldn't stand too close together or they risked looking like a couple. He handed the doorman two tickets. Kellen took one last deep breath and adjusted his tuxedo. The two friends walked through the huge entrance. Let the party begin.

***

As they walked in to the main hall, Kellen felt like a movie star. The entire place was decked out as if it was an after-party at the Oscars. Long, flowing sheets in white and black hung from the ceiling. Ice sculptures of famous scientists adorned every corner. A huge, golden banner sparkled above the stage announcing the Tenth Annual Science Banquet hosted by JonasTech. The company had spared no expense. Tables had been arranged in neat rows and decorated with lavish, floral arrangements. Off to the left was an annexe that had become a bar for the evening and to the right was a similar one that housed the buffet table. Waiters and waitresses buzzed about the room serving canapés and champagne. Kellen grabbed a glass of bubbly from a pretty-looking waitress. This is awesome, he concluded. He could feel Dan felt the same way. At this point, Dan was edging the both of them towards the bar. Kellen and Dan were both underage to drink, but it seemed to be the main place for the guests to congregate, so Kellen allowed himself to be led by the elbow.

The bar had been decorated in a similar fashion to the rest of the hall, with the black and white theme. At one end sofas had been laid out behind a thin silk curtain to give it some privacy. Kellen could only imagine what might go on behind there after the speeches and the party began. Scientists may appear prim and proper, but give them booze and it's like feeding Gremlins after midnight; they go wild. Although at that moment the guests appeared to be conducting themselves in an appropriate manner. In fact, everyone looked very smart, with the men in tuxedos and the women in beautiful, flowing dinner dresses – many of which were very low cut. He gave the room a quick scope, hoping to spot Linzi. But he couldn't see her. His spirits sank. Dan was too busy conversing with two young women to help him find her.

Kellen had always been too shy for random encounters with attractive women so he left Dan to it. They looked way out of his league, but they seemed to be enjoying the conversation. Good luck, Kellen thought, as he made his way back to the main hall leaving behind the cacophony of different conversations. He could feel that he was getting nervous again. What if she's not here? Just because her father was the guest speaker it didn't mean she would come to see him give his speech. He needed some air. He had been feeling strange since the cab journey. It's just nerves, he reiterated to himself.

As Kellen walked through the hall he wasn't paying attention to where he was going. His mind was preoccupied. He accidentally bumped in to someone. It was Linzi. Oh my God, he thought. Quick, think.

"I—I—I'm so sorry," he stammered. "I—I didn't see you. So sorry." His face had gone a bright scarlet. He could feel his cheeks burning.

Linzi returned a sweet smile and giggled. "It's okay. I wasn't paying attention either." She put her hand on Kellen's arm.

Kellen felt a surge of emotion rush through his body like electricity. She was even more beautiful up close. She was wearing a gorgeous, pastel-blue dress that flowed with the curves of her trim body. Her raven-coloured hair cascaded over her shoulders, ending at the small of her back. Her dark, hazel eyes dazzled in the light. She looked at Kellen and smiled. He realised he was staring and so promptly averted his gaze. There was a sweet, awkward moment when both were too shy to speak.

Linzi was the first to break the silence.

"You're Kellen Amos, aren't you? You sit at the back in the class."

She knows my name and where I sit, he realised. I'm going to puke. Stay calm. Answer, dummy. "Y—Yeah, that's me, yep." He was failing fast. He had to think of something to say. "H—How do you find the class?" Stop stammering, he suggested to himself.

"Umm... It's good. I took AP physics because my dad wanted me to. I enjoy it, but sometimes it can be really boring, especially if you've covered the subject countless times. I also never realised just how advanced AP physics was."

"Yeah, tell me about it!" Kellen exclaimed. He loved Professor Drake's class, but he didn't want to seem like the teacher's pet. "Dr Rollingson is your father, right?" he asked, attempting to steer the conversation to a new topic.

"That's right. He's the guest speaker tonight."

"Yeah, I saw that. I admire his work on space exploration very much," Kellen explained.

He took a sip of champagne. His hand for some reason was itching. He used to suffer from hives as a child, which would come out when he was under extreme stress or nervousness. He silently prayed that wasn't happening now.

"Oh, really? If you'd like I can introduce you later?" Linzi replied.

Kellen couldn't believe it. Here he was, chatting to the woman of his dreams and she was offering to introduce him to his idol. He felt the nervousness wash away. He was about to answer when a blond-haired guy walked over.

He kissed Linzi on the cheek and stood next to her with his arm around her. The boyfriend. He was a big guy with a definite athletic physique. His facial features were strong with a well-defined chin. Kellen had to admit, the guy did look dashing. They stared at each other. It was like watching two male lions on a nature program. The alpha male was definitely marking his territory. Feeling the tension building, Linzi tried to quell it. "Honey, this is Kellen Amos. He's in my class at school. I've offered to introduce him to my father."

The stranger smiled and reached out, offering Kellen his hand. "Hi. Casper Jackson. Pleasure to meet you," he said.

Kellen shook his hand and returned the smile. He really wanted to dislike Casper, but he seemed to be a genuinely nice guy. The awkwardness was back. A few seconds passed before Dan stumbled over to them.

"Yo, guys. Wassup?" he asked in his jovial tone. He looked at Linzi. "Ahh. You must be Linzi? Enchanté, madame." He took her hand and kissed it. Kellen and Casper both rolled their eyes. Linzi just laughed.

"We best find our table," Casper informed them. He and Linzi started to drift away when Linzi stopped and turned to Kellen.

"We're seated at the VIP table with my father, and some people couldn't make it. Would you like to join us? I'm sure no one will mind." She asked.

Before Kellen could answer, Dan butted in. "We'd love to."

Linzi smiled and then linked arms with Casper. Kellen and Dan followed. Other guests were also beginning to take their seats. He was excited about spending some time with Linzi, but Kellen didn't know if he could bear to watch her fawn all over her boyfriend for the evening. He would just have to be a man and put up with it.

As they reached the table, a tall, handsome young man rose off of his seat and gently pecked Linzi on the cheek. "Miss Rollingson. It's a pleasure to meet you again. May I say you're looking more stunning than ever?" The man put on his most seductive voice. "I hope I'll be having the pleasure of your company?"

Linzi just smiled and sat next to Casper. There was something about this man that made Kellen's skin crawl. So that must be the famous Mr Jonas, he realised. He was the CEO of the world's biggest research and development company. He was also stinking rich and owned half the city.

Kellen sat next to Dan. The Tenth Annual Science Banquet was underway.

***

The food was delicious. Waiters had been coming non-stop with silver trays covered in various dishes. Dan had tucked straight in to his food. The rest of the table, however, had been somewhat more reserved. Mr Jonas had played the part of host to perfection. His anecdotes and comments caused frequent laughter to erupt from the table. He was used to these social functions. He hated public events; ever since childhood he had been plagued by a fear of crowds, but by hosting them it made the company look good and it gave him a chance to do some much-needed networking with clients. He found himself intrigued by the young man sitting opposite. There was something under the shy exterior.

"So, Mr Amos, are you enjoying the banquet?"

"Yes, thank you. JonasTech has done a marvellous job," Kellen replied. He was trying not to be noticed by the man.

"I'm glad. And you're a scientist I take it?"

It felt to Kellen like he was being interrogated. "Yes. I'm on a physics scholarship at the Zygonia School of Excellence."

"Tremendous. And your grades are good?"

"They're okay." They could be better, Kellen thought. He was about to say so when Linzi spoke up.

"Only okay! He's just being modest, Mr Jonas. Kellen is actually top of his class." She looked at Kellen with a picturesque smile. His face went bright red again.

"Really," Jonas purred. It was a statement rather than a question. "Maybe you should work for me. The company is offering a summer internship this year. It'll provide you with an opportunity to work with some of the top scientists in your chosen field." He paused to let the offer sink in. "Think about it," he added, then turned away to listen to Dr Rollingson on stage, who was about to give his speech.

He was about halfway through his discussion of a recently discovered planet when a well-dressed man came and whispered in Mr Jonas' ear. He did not look amused. Jonas waited for the man to leave before excusing himself from the table and making his way out of the hall.

Jonas followed his aide down the long corridor to his office. He was glad to get out. Usually he would just send a company representative. However, his PR manager had advised he should attend to improve his public appeal, especially if he wanted to win the upcoming mayoral election. Not that he would lose the election anyway, he thought. It was costing him a fortune to secure the appropriate endorsements; politics wasn't cheap. He gave a slight laugh. Soon he wouldn't have to worry about mere petty elections. His smile broadened.

Rapturous applause filtered down the hallway as Jonas and his aide rounded the corner. The aide opened the office door. Jonas stepped in.

The room was dark. A single window was the only source of light. Half hidden in the shadows stood a man that always made him shudder. He hid, not wanting to show his fear. His father had taught him to never show weakness to those beneath him. It was the only lesson of worth he had learnt.

Jonas gestured to his aide. "Leave us."

The aide closed the door firmly behind him. The room was soundproofed. Nobody would hear their conversation.

Mr Jonas sat down in the leather chair behind his huge antique desk. "Make it quick. I have guests."

A man stepped out of the shadows and walked towards the desk. "I regret to report, Mr Jonas, that test results appear negative."

***

By the time Mr Jonas returned to the main hall, the tables had been cleared away and a band had set up on stage. Kellen had finally gotten his wish. He was alone with Linzi. Casper had rushed off, saying that he had to get up early for lacrosse the following day. Linzi had been annoyed as she was starting her new part-time job at Hockton and Sons Jewellers. She had been hoping Casper would take her. She seemed to be okay now though. They were just waiting for Dr Rollingson to join them.

"So, do you think you'll take up Mr Jonas' offer?" Linzi asked.

"I don't know. Maybe."

It was a fantastic offer. He would have the chance to get some real hands-on experience. He could learn so much at JonasTech working with the best. It was the thought of working for Mr Jonas that was stopping him. He was very charming and polite, but it appeared to Kellen to be a little too forced, as if it was an act. There was something very sinister about him.

"I'll have to think about it," he added.

"It would be a great opportunity for you. You really are good at physics. I wish I was."

"Your grades are good, aren't they?" Kellen asked. This could be his chance.

"They aren't as good as my dad would like," she said with a sigh.

"Maybe I could help you study."

"Really? That would be awesome. Thank you." She leant over and pecked Kellen on the cheek. He could feel the electricity from her touch. He was about to say something when Dr Rollingson walked towards them.

Linzi ran over and gave her father a huge hug. Kellen was still reeling from the kiss she had planted on his cheek. Now he was about to meet his idol. One of the most gifted minds on Earth and the foremost authority on space. He had only just discovered a new planet and published research on the possibility that it might contain life.

"Daddy, there's someone I'd like you to meet." She took the doctor by the arm and ushered him towards Kellen. "This is Kellen Amos."

"How do you do, young man? It's a pleasure to meet you." He gave Kellen a hearty handshake, which Kellen reciprocated.

"It's an honour, sir. I think your new article on Zepkus is amazing. I'm a real admirer of your work."

"Well, thank you. And you're a fellow physicist?" he asked, raising an eyebrow.

"Kellen is top of our class, Daddy. He's offered to tutor me." Linzi informed her father.

Kellen could feel his face burning again, although he was beginning to wonder if it were being caused by something other than embarrassment. The itch on his hand had turned in to an incessant burning sensation. He really didn't feel too good.

"I see. So you must know my good old friend, Professor Drake. We studied at Cambridge together." He turned around as the professor was coming over to join them. "Drake, you didn't tell me you had such delightful students."

Professor Drake laughed. "Mr Amos here is a very gifted young man. But his concentration lets him down." He looked at Kellen with a raised eyebrow. "By the way, how is your experiment going?"

Kellen didn't go red this time. His face went as white as snow in a blizzard.

The experiment! He'd left it running when he had been distracted by Dan. The room swirled around him like a vortex. He felt faint. The trio standing with him were aiming concerned looks at him.

"Are you okay, Kellen?" Linzi asked.

"I—I'm fine. Just a little warm." He had to get back to the lab before anything disastrous happened. If it hadn't already. "If you don't mind I might shoot off now. I'm feeling a little tired."

With that, Kellen bolted out of the room leaving Linzi alone with the doctor and the professor.

Chapter Five

Kellen shot through the double doors of the main entrance like a man on fire. There was a biting chill in the air. Impervious to it, he rushed down the steps in a blind panic, almost bowling over a courting couple as he launched himself down the remaining few steps. He paused to look at his watch. Eleven p.m. The lab would be closed by now. That meant he would either have to sneak in or bribe campus security to let him in. Professor Drake's going to flip if he finds out I left a running experiment, he thought. With that spurring him on, he bolted off down the street.

Three blocks away, he was gasping for breath. His lungs were on fire and his legs may as well have been jelly for all the use they were. Perspiration poured off his forehead, his clean white shirt soaked beneath his heavy dinner jacket. Jogging just didn't interest him much. Despite that he was an average sprinter, almost trying out for the school track team. That's it, I'm taking up that membership to the gym, he thought. He ripped off his bow tie and jacket. Then he ran like the wind.

"Hey, man. You dropped your stuff," shouted a homeless guy swigging a whisky bottle. Kellen took no notice.

He had to get back or something bad might happen. The super conducting serum was a potent, potentially unstable compound. If something went wrong, the ramifications could be huge. With that thought in his mind, he continued running.

He only managed to get one more block before he collapsed. His legs wouldn't carry him any further. He slumped down on a bench holding his head in his hands. Strangers out on the town looked at him with funny expressions on their faces. He didn't care what looks they gave him. He had failed. Not only that, he had broken a promise to Professor Drake and missed his opportunity to take Linzi home. He didn't know which was worse. The night that had been full of promise turned out to be a disaster. He had been a complete idiot for thinking he could run all the way back to his campus. In fact, he hadn't thought at all; he had simply run. He had never felt so dumb. He just prayed the equipment was okay and that someone had come in to switch it off. Deep down he knew it would still be running though. Scientists didn't touch other people's experiments unless they were asked to. It was like an unwritten rule. He had to get back before Professor Drake went to the lab. Kellen considered a taxi, but they would all be either on jobs or parked downtown cleaning puke off the back seats by now. Downtown was closer than the school campus, but Kellen had no energy left to move. The sweat-covered shirt was making him cold with the night air. He was beginning to wish he hadn't discarded his jacket so recklessly. Another mistake to add to the list, he supposed. It was hopeless.

Minutes that seemed endless ticked by. Not one cab had passed him. It felt as though he was in a ghost town. A group of girls behind him started to giggle. He looked up.

Down the street a small ice cream van was hurtling towards him, the tune of *Teddy Bears' Picnic* floating by on the breeze. For a second he thought he must be dreaming. Why would someone sell ice cream at this hour? It screeched to a halt right in front of him.

"Hop aboard the Halladay express!" Dan's chubby features popped out of the window. He was munching on an ice cream cone. "Hungry?" he asked, grinning.

I'm saved, Kellen thought, as he leapt to his feet. "What the… How'd you get that?"

"Never reveal your secrets, my friend. I got the feeling you were in a hurry. I knew you wouldn't get far, so I…" Dan paused, searching for the right word to use. "Acquired it!"

"You stole it?" Kellen asked, shocked.

"No. More like borrowed. I'll take it straight back, I promise. Although, it is a babe magnet. Bonjour, ladies." He winked at the group of girls who were still giggling at the strange sight. Dan switched his attention back to his stranded friend. "You coming or not?"

Kellen rushed around to the passenger door and jumped in. It felt surreal. The monotonous tune was still blaring out of the speakers as the truck peeled off, speeding towards the campus.

***

Kellen thought it was probably best that they didn't pull up right outside the lab in an ice cream van playing nursery rhymes. It was going to be hard enough as it was to get the security to let him in; he could do without them thinking he was some drunk nutcase trying to break in. So, he suggested Dan park the van by the dorm and the duo would walk over to the lab. It was a beautiful night for star gazing as there was a complete absence of cloud. But he didn't have the time.

As they strolled past the library, Dan stopped and tugged Kellen's elbow. "Yo, dude, what's the plan?" His voice had become a hoarse whisper.

"There isn't one!" Kellen replied. "Unless you got one?"

"Well now you mention it. Just follow my lead."

Dan marched straight up to the main entrance of the lab, loudly clearing his throat. It caused the guard in his booth to jump. He had been reading a dirty magazine and now stood red-faced. He hadn't realised that anyone would be around this time of night.

"Good evening, my good fellow. What a glorious night this is," Dan said, putting on a fake British accent. "My partner and I need access to the lab, wot-wot. If you could be so kind?"

Kellen rolled his eyes. This was never going to work.

"Sorry, no can do, sir. This lab is off limits to any unauthorised personnel. You'll have to come back tomorrow."

Dan put on a look of outraged shock. "This is preposterous. Do you not know who this man is? He is…" Dan had to stop to try and think of a famous British person. Got it. "Tony Blair! Former PM under her gracious majesty, Queen Elizabeth II of Great Britain."

The redneck guard would never know otherwise. He looked puzzled at Kellen, who gave a sheepish wave in return. The guard was about to object when Dan continued with his tirade.

"He has been invited by the great Professor Drake himself; founder of this very laboratory. Now kindly admit us, or I will be forced to report your…" He pointed to the guards XXX magazine sprawled on the floor. "Extra activities to your superiors. Big, busty Asians I believe? Outrageous!"

The guard stood for a few seconds contemplating his possible fate if he denied the two men entrance. Kellen's heart froze. The guard came out from behind his desk, put his electro-key in the lock and turned it. The glass door slid open. "Okay, but you gotta be quick," the guard informed them.

"Your secret is safe with me, my good man." Dan gave the guard a huge pat on the back. "We shall be mere moments. Mr Blair, follow me, wot-wot!"

Kellen obliged, keeping his eyes firmly fixed on the floor. He rounded the corner with Dan and waited for them to be well out of earshot of the guard before saying anything.

"How the hell did you pull that off?"

"With my pure genius and superb acting talent of course," Dan replied with a look of sheer satisfaction.

They walked at double speed down the long corridor. Kellen wasn't too sure about Dan's superb acting talent, but he was beginning to believe he was a genius. It was the second time that night he had saved him from utter failure.

"I don't know what I'd do without you. You're a good friend, Dan."

"Yeah, I know," he smiled back as they reached the correct lab.

Kellen tapped the key code in to the data pad. He told Dan to wait for him in the corridor. It was possible the security guard might come looking for them. Dan reluctantly agreed, but was disappointed he wouldn't get to use his hacking skills again. He felt like a spy in his tuxedo. Kellen entered the lab.

As the door sealed behind him, his worst nightmare was realised. The green liquid had bubbled up over the container in to a huge, boiling, putrid mass. It was all over the expensive equipment Professor Drake had told him to use. It was a disaster zone.

Kellen rushed over to the power socket, navigating his way around the noxious puddles that were letting off a choking gas. His hand still itched. He reached out and pressed the switch.

His body was flung halfway across the room, landing in the green chemical. Thousands of volts coursed through his veins mixing with the chemicals he had absorbed earlier in the day. His molecular structure began to bond with the mixture. Kellen blacked out.

***

"Hey, Kellen. Wake up, buddy."

As soon as Dan had heard the loud boom, he had grabbed the nearest chair and slung it through the glass. He had managed to drag Kellen's body out in to the corridor.

"Come on, buddy. You got to wake up." He slapped him on the cheek then put his ear to Kellen's chest. Good. His heart was still beating and he was breathing. The dumb guard had dashed off to fetch help. "Kellen, dude. *Wake up!*" He struck harder. Kellen jolted awake, coughing and spluttering. Dan reminded himself to thank God later.

"Where am I? What happened?" Kellen asked. He felt strange. It was as if his whole body was vibrating. There was a constant tingling sensation on his skin and he had the taste of iron in his mouth.

"There was an accident. Are you hurt?" Dan looked to see if there were any obvious injuries. None. Not a single scratch. "Wow, you are one lucky dude. Can you walk?"

"I think so." Kellen stood, using Dan as a support. He opened his eyes to something he didn't expect.

He could see the entire electromagnetic spectrum. He could see the electricity all around him; in the walls, the floor, even small electrical waves in the air. The most stunning of all was the electricity emanating from his body. It was an awesome bright light, like a star. He could see Dan's natural electricity too. It wasn't as bright as his, but it was still there. He closed his eyes and shook his head. It was gone.

The two of them made their way to the main entrance. By the time they got outside Kellen could support himself. A dozen security guards came rushing towards them along with Vice Principal Danvers and Professor Drake. The vice principal charged inside with half the security team, including the redneck, to check the damage. Drake rushed over to Kellen. His face had turned white.

"What the hell happened? Are you injured?" The concern was evident in his tone. Worry furrowed his brow.

"I'm so sorry, Professor. I got distracted. I take full responsibility. Thankfully no one was hurt," Kellen reported, despite the fact he wasn't convinced he had come out of it the same as he went in. "I feel fine," he added.

He heard Professor Drake tell one of the men to cancel the ambulance before he turned his attention back to Kellen, who couldn't look the professor in the eyes. The disappointment was too acute in them. He had let his mentor down.

Vice Principal Danvers came charging back out. She took one look at Kellen and Dan. "If I find out either of you were directly involved in this…" She let the sentence hang in the air, full of menace, "I will personally pack your bags and ship you back home in a box."

The professor put his hand on her shoulder. "It's late," he said. "Why don't you let me deal with this for now?"

"Fine."

And with that, the vice principal stormed off.

Kellen let out a huge sigh of relief, but stopped it short. He noticed the professor's face was like thunder. He looked down at Kellen.

"You're lucky Miss Danvers and I have a good working relationship and that she trusts me to deal with you," he explained. "I want to see you in my office at ten a.m. No excuses. Go get some rest," Drake said, as he walked off leaving Kellen and Dan alone.

Feeling like a failure, Kellen headed off in the direction of his dorm alone. He was unaware that his destiny had been changed forever.

Chapter Six

Beep, beep, beep! Eight a.m. Kellen reached out a hand and slammed it down on the alarm clock. As it was about to make another annoying beep, he gave it a heavier whack, silencing it. The last thing he wanted was to get out of bed after experiencing one of the most restless nights of his life. Several times he had jumped out of bed feeling like his body was on fire, cold sweat dripping from his forehead like Niagara Falls. Time after time, the sounds of vomiting erupted from the bathroom. He'd never felt so ill. Now it was time to face the music with Professor Drake, which was another thing he didn't want to have to do. The look of disappointment had been plain on his face, a look which had haunted Kellen all through the night. He was surprised he managed to get any sleep at all. This wasn't going to be a good day.

He dragged himself out of bed and made his way to the bathroom, carefully plotting his course around his possessions. It was at the end of the hallway and shared by six other people. Thankfully at eight in the morning, he wouldn't have a problem with it being occupied.

He stood over the sink, looking in the mirror. He wasn't a bad looking guy, a bit geeky with his freckles, but that was all. His short dark-brown hair matched his deep hazel eyes. Shame having good looks didn't help his concentration, he thought bitterly.

Whilst considering his looks, Kellen went about his morning routine, all the time dreading his fate with the professor. Standing in the shower, his mind began drifting back to his restless night; the continuous burning sensation, the constant tingling in his hands, the unnerving sensation that he was vibrating. It had almost driven him insane. Despite the warm water from the shower, he began to shudder. He felt fine now, although he was acutely aware of a metallic taste in his mouth and the smell of what he thought to be burning sulphur. He considered it could just be his imagination, but still it was odd. Trying to ignore it, he reached over to switch off the shower. The hairs on his neck rose to attention.

Bang!

The entire shower unit had blown straight off the wall, exposing electrical cables beneath. Sparks went flying from Kellen's fingertips, hungry to reach for more electricity. He stood in horror not knowing what to do, the shower unit broken in to a million pieces. His mind was racing. He lifted his hands up to his face.

Bright white sparks were racing around his palm following the lines of his hand right to his fingertips. He could feel the raw power surging through his core and extending to his limbs. His right hand began to vibrate, causing more and more energy to build up. The pain was excruciating to the point where he collapsed to the floor, hunched over his arm in an attempt to stop whatever was happening. By now the electrical current was racing around his entire body. It was as if he had somehow become a conduit for the static electricity in the air. His body was absorbing it at an alarming rate. From what started as a tingling sensation, it had now grown exponentially to a small scale lightning storm in mere minutes. It frightened him. His body could only take so much before it gave out.

Brilliant yellow and blue streaks were jumping from his body creating burn marks all around the room. One spark had zapped the glass mirror, smashing it to pieces. He was covered in sweat. If I don't do something soon, I'll explode, he thought.

Fear racked his brain. With the pain he couldn't think straight. All he knew was he had to do something, people were beginning to stir down the corridor. What if they came in and saw him like this? What if he hurt them? His skin was burning and letting off a nauseating smell. He had to get out. But how?

"Are you okay in there?" a voice called from down the hall.

"I'm fine. Nothing to worry about," he shouted back, barely able to form the words.

He could hear footsteps edging towards the bathroom. Damn. Whoever it was obviously didn't believe him and was coming to check for themselves. He looked up. All around him he could see the electricity. He could even sense the person walking towards the bathroom; their bio-electricity was like a homing device in his mind, they stood out like a bright beacon. He didn't have much time.

A flash of inspiration hit him like a thunderbolt. Fighting through the pain, he tried focusing his mind on his hand. It was working. The electricity was congregating in his palm, so now all he needed to do was channel it. Taking a wild guess, he thrust his palm at the far window. A bolt of electricity shot forth and exploded through the window. Raw power still coursed through his veins and was beginning to build again. He wasn't only absorbing electricity, he was generating it.

"Are you sure you're okay?"

Kellen didn't bother to answer.

Boooom! He let off a huge sonic boom as he started to run; he was running at the speed of light. Nothing but a huge blur sped past his vision. Buildings, trees, cars, people. It was exhilarating and frightening at the same time. Faster and faster he ran. He could feel his body burning off the electricity that had built up inside him. But it was running out. Fast.

He couldn't find the breaks! His continuous running was burning off his reserves. Trees and fields still sped past him.

But then, without warning, he came to an abrupt halt, his entire body swaying in the middle of the field. Small sparks leapt excitedly in his eyes. His eyelids flickered. Then blackness.

*****

By the time Kellen woke up, he was shivering with the cold, naked except for a burnt towel around his waist. He had no idea how long he had been there. His head was pounding. Where is here? he wondered, taking a look around.

He found himself in the middle of a corn field. The sun had dropped behind some fluffy cotton clouds. It was daylight. He could still feel the electricity in his body, but it was nothing more than a slight irritation. He was expecting his body to be badly burnt, but there was nothing, not even a scratch. Trying to stand, his legs felt shaky and so he sat for a few moments to let himself adjust. He still had no idea where he could be.

As he sat, so many questions flooded his brain. He could absorb and generate electricity, which he could channel, that much was certain. But he had no idea if he could control it, or whether it was random. He was able to sense anything that was electrical, or generated electricity. He could also run at a tremendous speed it seemed. How did this happen? He could only assume it was a result of the accident; that kind of thing always occurred in the comic books he read. There was only one person who might be able to answer his questions; Professor Drake. He could be his only hope, but until Kellen found out where he was, there was nothing he could do except find a way home. He was dimly aware of some power cables running to his left. He decided if he followed those, they would lead him to a farm or something.

This time he managed to stand. The small burnt towel flapped gently in the breeze as he opened up his senses to the power cables. He could see them in his mind, running along a road; he could virtually taste the electricity. And there it was, a small farmhouse situated about a mile off. The electricity began to vibrate in his body again, so he began walking.

It didn't take him long to reach his destination, considering what he had been through. His body was feeling pretty strong, albeit a bit wobbly.

The farmhouse was only small. It was built of white-washed wood with a veranda and a screen door. To the left, there was a big red barn and a corn silo. Then Kellen spotted a fully laden washing line. Just what I need, he thought, stalking over to the line, praying there was no nearby guard dog. A bad experience as a child had left him petrified and with the way his luck was going, there was bound to be one. Thankfully, as he approached, there wasn't anything waiting to maul him, so he selected a pair of stone-wash jeans and a light grey, plaid shirt. He detested having to steal, but he made a vow he would bring the clothes back as soon as he could. Maybe a bit of Dan had rubbed off on him after all?

He was just buttoning up the shirt when he heard the screen door slam. He whipped around. The phrase, oh Holy crap, sprung to the forefront of his mind. Staring straight at him were two shotgun barrels.

"Hey, thief, git offa my land!" roared a grey-haired, middle aged man. "You got thirty seconds, scumbag, ta git."

"I'm sorry, sir. P—Please, I'll bring the clothes back." Kellen was beginning to back away from the guy. He looked mad.

"This is Kansas, boy. We don't lend clothes. Now git!" He fired a warning shot in to the air.

Kansas. He had run seven hundred miles from home. How am I going to get back? he thought. At this moment in time he didn't care. He was in danger. He had no doubts that the man would shoot him for trespassing and stealing; he could easily bury the body out here. Kellen ran for his life.

At first he ran as a normal human being. The vibrations in his body were building up tempo. Sparks began to fly. This is it. *Booom!*

He was off at light speed, leaving the farmer staring in awe.

***

Kellen made it to the city limits before he burnt out again. His borrowed clothes, unlike the towel, had remained virtually intact this time. Was he learning to control the amount of power he used by instinct? he wondered. A public clock announced it was ten. He was now officially late for his meeting. He had failed again.

His feeble attempt to control his new skills had left him feeling hungry and drained. All he wanted to do was sleep, but he couldn't, not until he knew more about his situation. He sat down on a bench to ponder.

He had shown that the powers were controllable, but to what extent, or how, he had no idea. When he found the power cables he had just opened up his senses. The second time he ran, he had just willed it the same as the lightning bolt in the bathroom. He had deduced that his super-speed could only be unleashed when there was enough power stored inside him, but so far that's all he could work out. He needed the professor. He had to know if he, or anyone else, was in danger. Kellen rose slowly off the bench, flexing his muscles. One more try, he thought.

With all his might he gathered the remaining electricity that he could feel in his body. He had no idea how to absorb, or create, more. It began to build. Exhilaration flashed in his eyes as he sped off down the street towards the school.

Seconds later, he burst in to the office, barely managing to stop. He had made it. At a cost. He looked around to see Professor Drake staring from behind his desk, mouth ajar. Kellen gave him a faint smile, tiny sparks still jumping from him.

"Sorry I'm late," he said faintly. "But I think I need your help." Then he collapsed in a heap on the floor.

Chapter Seven

The sun had set deep behind the horizon long before Kellen awoke. His body felt as though he had been put through a blender. Every muscle and sinew groaned with over-exhaustion. But at least he was alive. The day's events had terrified him and yet something inside him had started to accept that he was different now. A part of him even hoped it was permanent.

He sat himself up, scratching his head. The last thing he could remember was collapsing in the professor's office. Looking around, he found himself alone in a small side room, awards and certificates dotting the deep-red walls one end, whilst a mammoth bookshelf was housed along another. It was packed to the brim with books and strange pieces of equipment. The only source of light was a huge static electricity ball, its brilliant blue lightning forks creating a relaxing atmosphere. This must be the professor's bedroom when he's on campus, he thought, groaning as he stood.

The luminescent glow mesmerised him. He could taste the familiar metallic twang of electricity. The hairs on his body began to rise. It was as if the ball was luring him in; the constant hum whispering to him, urging him to touch it and be one with the electricity. It would be so easy. The current whispered to him. He would be free with no physical form to constrain him. He slowly reached out his hand, sweat dripping from his forehead. The electricity in the ball jumped around, reaching out to him.

"Kellen, no, don't!"

Kellen started, causing his body to twist around. His hand brushed against the ball. The electricity inside it went crazy. It bounced around inside, sending bolts of lightning streaking around the room. He could feel the pure elemental force climbing up his arm. The sheer power of it scared him. His body was absorbing it from the ball at an alarming rate; he could feel the energy storing in the centre of his body. He felt as though any moment he would explode.

"Son, you have to let go," Professor Drake called out.

Kellen couldn't hear him. He was losing himself to the electricity, wanting more than anything to be a part of the ball, to be absorbed by it and become one with the elements. His mind melded with the sheer force.

"Let go, Kellen."

He was dimly aware of a voice talking to him, a hand tugging at his shoulder trying to pull him off. He was lost, mesmerised by the dancing blue bolts. He wanted to join them in their wild ecstasy, forever being part of nature. No, wait, he thought. He didn't want to become part of nature. It was the electricity taking over his mind. There were things he had to do in the world.

He lifted his hand. A violent burst of energy erupted from the static electricity ball, hurtling Kellen and the professor across the room. Both of them smashed into the far wall, leaving them stunned and gasping for air. Professor Drake was the first to rise.

"Kellen, are you okay?"

"Yeah I'm fine, Professor. What the hell happened there?" Kellen asked, his mind reeling. His head was pounding, but his body felt great. There was no pain or weariness left in him; if anything he felt as though he could run a marathon.

"The ball is a constant-current source connected in parallel with a capacitor and a very large electrical resistance. It appears as though your body was absorbing the constant flow of static. When you let go, you were generating and sustaining electricity, which is why we ended up over here on the floor," Professor Drake explained, pulling his pupil up on his feet. "I think you need to tell me exactly what happened last night?"

Kellen didn't know where to begin, so he started his tale from the point where he had first been distracted by Dan. The frown on the professor's face revealed his disappointment. Kellen had to drop his gaze when he told him how they had tricked the guard into allowing them in the building, so that he could switch off the experiment before the professor realised.

Shame washed over him as he finished. The professor stood there silent.

"I'm sorry, Professor." It was all he could say.

"Yes, well, you've broken all the cardinal rules of science, not to mention school rules. You used substances you are unsure of, you left an experiment running without supervision, you lied your way in to the lab in order to cover up your mistakes and..." Professor Drake let the sentence trail off, taking a deep breath. "But that is not the issue. Get dressed and meet me out the front."

Kellen just stood there dumbfounded. He expected a much harsher tirade from his mentor. He was relieved that it hadn't materialised. The professor was about to leave the room.

"I *am* sorry, Professor, I didn't mean for all this to happen." He had no idea what was going to happen to him, but something inside him told him life would be very different from now on.

Professor Drake looked at him as though he could read the thoughts torturing his mind. "It's okay, we'll figure this out somehow. Get dressed."

Within five minutes, Kellen was dressed and ready to go. He took one final look at the Van der Graf generator sitting on the table. It was mesmerising, but this time he managed to look away, the realisation that he could've been lost forever bouncing around his brain. He closed the door behind him, hoping the professor would give him the answers he needed.

***

The Zygonia City shopping district was buzzing as usual. Hordes of shoppers were going about their business, oblivious to the gorgeous but unusual weather the region had been experiencing of late. The hum of excited conversations filled the air as Linzi made her way through the busy crowds towards the jewellers on the corner of Hammond and Rochester.

She had finally managed to get a part-time job to bring in a little extra money. Her father sent her an allowance every week, which she was grateful for. But she wanted to prove that she could make her own way in the world, even if it was only a weekend and after-school job. Her dream was to go to college out of state to study drama. If she could prove that she could take care of herself, it would strengthen her argument when it came around to telling her father that she wanted to move away. It's not like he wasn't used to her being away. She'd been at boarding school for four years already.

She found herself smiling as she walked along the street. Everything would work out fine. All she needed to do was get through the first day.

As she walked towards the jewellers, she spotted a news stand. The headline announced the museum robbery. According to one paper, police were baffled as to the culprit; not only was it a robbery, but there had been murder too.

Linzi shuddered. How could anyone commit murder? Zygonia was a beautiful, bustling city. This end of town appeared to be void of any criminal activity and she hoped it would stay that way. Intrigued though, she bought a copy of the paper and continued on her way, dodging hurried shoppers as she went. It appeared that three of the robbers had been murdered. A fourth had been picked up by the police. Somehow, one of the new exhibits had still managed to disappear. It looked like a professional hit and police were asking for witnesses to come forward and for Zygonian citizens to remain vigilant. Linzi hoped it was a one-off, but a deep-rooted doubt came creeping in to her mind that the Zygonia City crime rate was on the brink of soaring. After all, there had been an increase in the number of muggings in the city; the police were too useless to stop those spilling over into more high profile crimes.

She read as she walked. It didn't take her long to reach the jewellers. It was situated along the main road surrounded by tall office buildings and swanky restaurants. The jewellers itself was relatively small in comparison to the surroundings. To any visitor of the city, the building would look out of place, but it had been there for years and most of the buildings surrounding it were owned by the same company. In fact, most of the shopping district was owned by Hocktons. Two security men were positioned outside the main entrance, both old and who looked like they should have been pensioned off years ago. She imagined they would be no good against hardened criminals, but she guessed they were there to put the rich customers at ease. If only I could afford to shop here, she thought, as she made her way around to the staff entrance at the rear of the building.

Despite the appearance of poor security, inside was a different story. Being a new member of staff, she had to go through various checks before being shown her duties by the section manager. It was a pretty mundane job being stuck behind a counter, but Linzi was grateful to be earning a bit of extra money and the rest of the staff seemed to be friendly enough. This was a place she felt she could be happy working.

***

Linzi's shift seemed to drag on forever and yet when she turned to the clock, it was only 12.48. Most of the time she just stood behind the counter daydreaming and tapping her fingers on the bright, polished surface, willing the time to move faster so that she could get out and go and see Casper. Their two families had been friends for as long as she could remember. They'd grown up together. It hadn't been until one of the many family functions last summer that they realised they were more than just friends. At first, they'd kept their relationship a secret, not knowing whether her father would like the fact that she was dating a guy four years older than herself. But Casper had turned out to be an amazing boyfriend. Her father wasn't happy with the situation but realised his daughter was happy. Something she hadn't been since the death of her mother. Not that Casper seemed to pay much attention to her these days; all he seemed to care about was winning the Lacrosse Championship and graduating next summer. She hoped the new lingerie she had bought would change that. But she doubted it.

"You can have your break in ten minutes," her battleaxe of a supervisor informed her, breaking her out of another daydream. She was the only person working in the shop that Linzi wasn't sure of.

"Okay. How long do I get?"

"An hour, no longer."

With that, the woman disappeared into the back of the shop.

One whole hour, Linzi thought, trying to seem enthusiastic. She wanted the job, but not if it stayed like this; her opportunity to prove herself was not living up to her hopes and expectations after all. Out of the handful of customers that had come in, each had gone to a familiar face to be served.

"Don't worry, it gets better," Peter said.

"Thank you. How did you know what I was thinking?"

"Oh, honey, with a face as long as yours, a blind nun could tell. It was like that when I first started. Just smile, it draws the customers in."

"Really?" she asked, willing to learn any new trick she could to help her out.

"Of course. Here comes a handsome guy, give it a go."

Linzi felt stupid, but she put on the warmest smile she could muster. More shoppers had filtered in to the shop, each wearing a long coat and dark sunglasses. She frowned, but took little notice of them, as she caught the attention of one of the shoppers who was walking straight for her. Only five minutes left then she could go on her break, but she desperately wanted to make her first sale.

"Hello, can I help you?"

Her heart sunk. The old battleaxe had stolen her sale. Now she would go off to lunch having done nothing all morning. She sighed, closing up her till. There would be plenty more opportunities for her to improve her financial situation with commission, she hoped, walking over to one of her new colleagues to let them know she would be going now. There was a lot she could do in an hour. The weather outside was gorgeous and she wanted to make the most of it.

As she walked over to the door, one of the customers stepped in front of her, barring the entrance to the shop.

"Can I help you, sir?"

"Yeah, sure you can," the man replied. Licking his lips, he removed his sunglasses and began devouring her with his eyes.

Linzi felt the hairs on the back of her neck prick up. "Well I'm just going on my break I'm afraid. I'm sure one of the other assistants will be happy to serve you." There was no way she was going to, commission or not.

"Sorry, sweetheart, but I can't let anybody leave."

"What? If you'll excuse me please, sir." He had backed her up against a counter. She could feel her heart thumping. Peter caught her eye and made a move forwards to see what was going on.

One of the long coated men whipped out a shotgun, cracking Peter over the head. As his chin slammed against the counter on his way to the floor, an audible crunch indicated his jaw had been broken. He slumped to the floor.

"Okay, we don't want any trouble. Just do as we say and nobody else will get hurt."

The other men in coats pulled out similar weapons. There were several gasps from staff and customers alike while one of the men locked the door and the others began taking handbags and any valuables. A couple of women almost fainted at the sight of the guns. The manager, Mr Phelps, came out from the back of the shop.

"What's happening here?" he asked, his eyes wide open with fear as he spotted the shotguns.

The man that appeared to be the leader laughed. "What do you think we're doing old man?" He looked around and opened his arms wide. "We're robbing the joint."

"Oh my dear goodness," Mr Phelps said, the words tumbling out of his mouth in disbelief. He shuffled around to the front of the counter, joining other terrified bodies in the shop. "Please everybody remain calm, I'm sure this will be over shortly."

The coated men laughed. "Listen to the man, nobody try any heroics."

Screw that, Linzi thought, bringing up her knee sharply into the midsection of the man barring her way. The air was forced out of his lungs as he collapsed forward, bent over double and groaning on the floor. She took her moment.

Leaping behind the counter, she slammed her hand down on the button to trigger the silent alarm system. A rough hand yanked her backwards.

"So we got ourselves a feisty one," the leader of the group sneered at her. "That was a dumb move. Everybody into the back. Now!"

The man slung Linzi across the room by the scruff of her neck, only for her to fall in a heap in one corner of the storage room. Two more armed men were back there; the security guards had already been tied up.

She shot the leader a fierce look. "You won't get away with this. The police'll be here any second."

He scratched his bearded chin. "I guess you're right about that, missy." He turned to look at the armed men gathered behind him. "Load up, boys. Looks like we got ourselves a hostage situation."

***

Kellen sat on the cold surface of the worktop, waiting for the professor to return. They had been here for nearly three hours running various tests on his body, some of which had been very unpleasant. To him, it had seemed as though Professor Drake enjoyed the uncomfortable ones a little too much. Kellen knew he had let him down but was determined to make it up to him.

Just as he was buttoning up his shirt, the professor returned with a long sheet of paper, his eyes peering over the top of his glasses, as he mulled over the latest test results.

"It appears as though you're molecular structure has somehow reacted to the chemical you were using in your experiment," he informed Kellen, without looking up from the piece of paper.

"Is it permanent?"

"I would imagine so, yes. When you were electrocuted it mixed with the chemical in your bloodstream and has completely rewritten your biological make-up."

"And in English that means?"

Professor Drake gave him a stern look. "It means the electricity has bonded with your atomic structure. The chemical has made it become part of you."

Wow, he thought, sliding himself off of the table. There was no way he had been expecting that. What did it all mean? How would this change his life? Was he in danger? So many questions plagued him, he didn't know where to begin.

He walked over to the window and looked out. Life had seemed so much simpler only twenty-four hours ago. Now it was one gigantic mess with him stuck right in the middle. Nothing was ever going to be the same again.

"Am I in any danger?" he asked, wanting to know the outcome of his stupidity.

"I'm not too sure. If you absorb too much electricity then there's a possibility your body could break down at an atomic level. You saw what happened back in my office."

Kellen had tried to push that out of his mind. It would have been so easy to just let himself go, absorbing the electricity and disappearing forever. A part of him wished he had now. The professor joined him at the window.

"This doesn't have to be a curse," he said, taking Kellen by the shoulders and looking him straight in the eye. "I believe you're going to have the most amazing abilities. In a way, you've defied all the laws of nature. You're a scientific marvel."

"But how? I don't feel like anything except a failure."

"We'll train. With a little control, who knows what you can achieve. Tell me, Kellen, what have you discovered you can do so far?"

Over the next half an hour, he explained to Professor Drake how he could absorb the electricity around him and build up vibrations in his body to make him run faster than anything on the planet; he told him of how he could generate lightning bolts to fling out of his hands and how he could see differing levels of the electromagnetic spectrum, including bio-electricity given off by a living object; and finally he told him how he could sense sources of electromagnetic energy if he really concentrated.

"I think my body stores all of the energy for me to use as and when I need to, but it's really hard to figure out how to use each different ability."

Professor Drake paced around the room in thought. Eventually he looked up. "If you say you can detect different sources of electromagnetic energy, I wonder if you can pick up different radio waves in the air?"

"I can see them," Kellen explained. "But I'm not sure I can do anything else with them."

"Give it a go, concentrate, see if you can hear them."

The professor seemed almost giddy with excitement. Kellen wasn't sure what he was supposed to be doing, but after all the disappointment he had caused, he thought it best to try anyway. He closed his eyes, questing for the electrical signal of a radio wave. There was nothing.

"I can't do it, Professor."

"Concentrate harder, boy. Listen with your mind."

He did as the professor asked, his head pounding with the effort. Any minute, he thought, I'm going to pass out. Very faintly, he could hear the buzz of static, not in his ears, but inside his skull. He locked on to the signal, concentrating harder to make it clearer. Within seconds he was bopping away to the sounds of his favourite radio station.

"Professor, I did it. I can hear the radio in my head."

"There you go," Professor Drake replied, a smile on his face. "A little concentration goes a long way."

Kellen wasn't listening any more. He had become lost in his newfound ability, dancing around the room with a new lightness in his step. This is awesome, he thought, swooping past the professor, who seemed as equally amused. Perhaps this wouldn't be so bad after all.

"I wouldn't get too carried away just yet, not until you have more experience of using these new abilities."

Still the dancing continued, with Kellen not taking a blind bit of notice. He was far too excited to stop. The song finished and so did his dancing. He continued to listen to the radio in his head. There was a news report. He listened intently to the words of the newscaster, the broad smile on his face dropping further with every syllable.

Breaking news. Several armed men have taken the staff and customers of Hockton and Sons Jewellers downtown. As of yet, the police believe that no one has been harmed, but witnesses have claimed they heard gunshots. Nobody can get close enough to the building to truly find out what's happening. Citizens are urged to stay clear of the area. We'll have more updates as they come in.

Kellen turned to Professor Drake, his face drained of colour. That was Linzi's employers, he realised. His heart pounded in his chest and his breath came in rapid bursts. The professor dashed over to him.

"I told you not to overdo it. Are you okay?" he asked, his voice overflowing with concern.

"I'm fine, Professor, but I have to go."

He stepped around the professor, who stood there completely unaware of what was going on. He grabbed Kellen by the sleeve. "Why are you going? There's more testing to be done. We have no idea if this is doing any damage to you."

Right now, Kellen didn't care if it was. He was the only one capable of getting in to the jewellers and rescuing Linzi. He wrestled with his conscience as to whether to tell the professor what was going on. After a few seconds, he decided it was best. "There's a hostage situation downtown. Keep an ear to the radio and you'll get the results of your test."

"You're in no fit state to go off being a hero. You've had no training and know very little about how to control your powers. Somebody could get seriously injured, including you." His eyes implored Kellen to stay and rethink his rash decision, but it was too late, the look on his face said his mind had been made. Drake sighed. "You're not going to listen to me, but you also can't afford anybody seeing you use your powers. Make sure you hide your face."

"I will, Professor. I promise."

And then he was gone in the blink of an eye, leaving the professor standing alone in the lab, pride and concern filling his face in equal measure.

"Please be careful, Kellen," he said, leaving the lab to go and find a radio.

***

The hostages had been locked in a tiny office at the back of the building for what seemed like hours. Only one man watched over them, his eyes periodically leering at Linzi. Most of them were huddled in groups on the floor, some weeping, some with a grim determination to get through this clear on their faces. A single window was the only access to the outside world, but none of them could see anything out of it. All any of them could do was listen to the frenzy going on outside and the constant sound of police sirens.

Linzi picked at the threads of the worn-out grey carpet next to her, trying to occupy her mind. Every time the man at the door looked at her, she came back at him with a defiant glare. If only there was something she could do to get them out of this, she thought. Any action would only get someone killed. There was no way she could take on the armed men on her own. She felt helpless.

Peter's prone body lay next to her, the back of his hair matted with dried blood from the wound on his head. He let out a faint moan, which made the rest of the hostages stir uncomfortably.

She looked out of the window, blinking as she did. For a second she thought she had seen a masked face staring in. It had to have been a mistake, a trick of the mind. One of her teachers had taught the class about how people can see and hear things under extreme situations that weren't really there. This could be classed as an extreme situation, she thought, getting up on her feet.

The guard stepped toward her. "What're ya doing?" he asked, pointing the shotgun right at her.

"Take it easy there. I'm just going over to the window."

The guard nodded and so she went to take a closer look. The burning heat from the sun coming through the window was magnified as she got closer. Her eyes squinted until they adjusted to the bright light. She took in a sudden breath.

There was the face again, plain as day underneath the windowsill, the masked eyes staring straight at her. It was a man, dressed like something out of a comic book, with his black eye-mask hiding his identity. There was something familiar about him though. She had no time to think about it as the guard was coming towards her to see what she was looking at. She whipped around to face him, her back to the window.

"What're ya looking at out there?"

"Nothing, there's nothing out there to see except sky and the sun," she replied, giving the man a flirtatious smile while her fingers fiddled with the lock on the window.

He returned the smile. "You don't fool me," he said, roughly shoving her aside so that he could see for himself. He turned back to her. Linzi prayed the face had gone. He snorted. "Stay away from the window."

Suddenly it flew open, a hand reached up and landed on the guard's shoulder. The guard writhed in agony as bolts of electricity crisscrossed around his body. He slumped to the floor accompanied by the thud of the gun as it hit the deck. The masked hero hopped into the room, closing the window behind him. He smiled at the bewildered faces that greeted him.

"I'm here to rescue you."

Seconds ticked by before anyone realised what was going on. Linzi was the first to make a move forward.

"Who are you?"

Kellen needed to think of a name fast. His powers seemed to be centred around electricity. Electro Boy? No, that was too lame, he thought. The faces in the room looked at him in awe and anticipation. He needed something catchy. "Call me… Voltage."

Having an alias awakened his dream of being a hero. As a young boy he had read comic book after comic book about men with amazing powers that became heroes. Now he was one of them, except *he* was real. The new identity gave him an incredible boost of confidence. Moving to the centre of the office, he decided it was time to take charge. The rest of the armed men could burst in at any moment. He couldn't afford to waste a second.

"How many men are there?" he asked, aiming the question at Linzi.

"I don't know, but they're all out in the front of the shop."

Damn, not knowing the exact number would make it a lot more dangerous to just go out there half-cocked. He opened his mind up, stretching to feel for the men's bodies, concentrating until he locked on to them.

Linzi watched Voltage with a sense of amazement. Half of her was nervous as hell about what was going to happen now, but the other half was equally as excited. Whoever he was, he was a handsome man, she thought, wanting to find out more about him.

He opened his eyes and came towards her. "I need you to make sure everyone stays here. No matter what happens, don't come out of this room." He looked around at the frightened faces. Linzi was the only hostage that didn't seem afraid. "In ten minutes, I want you to lead these people outside. The police will be there waiting."

"Why? Where are you going?"

"To save the day, of course," he said, giving her a wink and a smile.

Her bio-electrical aura flared. A sudden burst of confidence washed over him again. He bent down and kissed her, feeling her warm lips press against his. There was no resistance. They parted and in the blink of an eye, he was gone, out of the door, leaving Linzi standing alone, wanting to chase after him.

Within a second he was in the front of the shop, smack bang in the middle of the bewildered men. Each one looked at the other, as if one of them would have the answer as to where this guy came from all of a sudden.

Kellen just smiled at them. "Hi, guys. Didn't anybody ever tell you guns could kill?"

"Who the hell are you?" one of the men asked with a growl.

"I'm the new sheriff in town, and you guys are going down."

Kellen burst around the room, using his super-speed to overwhelm the armed robbers. He zipped and whizzed, sending guns and bodies flying through the air. In the blink of an eye, only two armed men remained. Both of them stood there dumbstruck, neither one of them knowing what to do next.

Kellen just laughed. "That the best you can do?"

The leader of the group motioned to a well-framed man next to him. "Don't just stand there, you idiot, grab him before he can do it again."

The man lunged, but Kellen sidestepped so that the large man tumbled into the glass cabinet behind him. It smashed, sending jewellery sprawling out across the marble floor. Now there was only one left.

He squared off against Kellen, raising his shot gun straight for Kellen's head. "You son of a—" He never finished the sentence.

Kellen had thrust out his palm. A tiny lightning bolt flew out, stunning the final assailant. He sunk to the floor like the *Titanic* with a dull thud.

Kellen had done it; he had managed to save the day without anybody getting hurt. Not only that, he had kissed the girl of his dreams as well. The memory of the kiss made his cheeks flush red as he whipped around the room checking for pulses on the fallen men. They were fine, just fast asleep. Being a hero was fun, he mused, wondering if he should open the door to announce himself to the city's media. He decided it was best to leave without a fuss and get back to the professor. But first he needed to let the police know the hostages were safe.

He sent out his senses again, searching for the police radio frequency. Having done it a few times now, it was getting easier to pick out what he was looking for. It only took him a second to find it.

"Come in," he said, not knowing if anybody would pick up on the other end.

Who is this?

He could hear the voice in his head. He wasn't sure if he was ever going to get used to that feeling. "The hostages are safe now. You can come in and get them out."

Repeat, who is this? You're on a private frequency.

The corners of his mouth turned up into a grin. "Call me…" He paused for dramatic effect. "Voltage!"

With that, he shot out of the rear entrance into the glaring sunshine. Having these powers wasn't a curse, they were a blessing. Now he could really do something with his life; make a difference like he had always wanted to. He was a hero now. And he was loving every second.

Chapter Eight

The JonasTech headquarters was situated in the heart of the industrial zone of Zygonia City. The main tower in the centre of the complex stood tall, its shadow stretching out over the other smaller high-rise buildings; the sharp, rectangular shape and black tinted windows of the tower made it look more like an obsidian obelisk rather than a centre for science and innovation. At its peak sat the logo of the company glinting as the bright morning sun reflected off its rotating golden surface. Everybody knew the building by sight. But nobody knew the dark secrets held within its depths. Except for one man.

Jonas sat behind his polished, oak desk in his office on the ninety-sixth floor, his jaw clenched tight as he read the day's news. *Masked hero foils yet another robbery: still has time to save kitten*, read the headline in bold print across page one. *Anti-vigilante mobs roam streets*, read another. He smiled.

Putting the newspaper down, he rose from his black leather chair and strolled over to the glass window that spanned the entire wall behind him. From up here, he could survey the entire city that lay beneath him. It was an industrial marvel of the modern age, with its tall buildings, hover trams, shopping malls and state-of-the-art tourist attractions. To men of lesser stature it must have been a humbling sight, but Jonas just sneered at it. If all went according to plan then the whole panorama before him would be his. With the wealth left to him by his father, he was already one of the most powerful men in society. But he wanted more. He wanted to own it all and crush it beneath his shining black shoe. There was only one thing that might stop him.

He moved away from the window and walked towards the large portrait of his father. When Mr Jonas Senior was alive, this had been his office. After his untimely death, Jonas Junior had inherited it and made a few minor alterations. He pressed a button underneath the picture, stepping back to watch the image of his father fade to black, only to be replaced by the fuzz of static on a screen. The communicator hummed for a few seconds before it was picked up at the other end.

"Mr Jonas," Pulse greeted him.

The two men rarely wasted many words on one another. If Jonas had his way, his father's creepy old bodyguard would be done away with. But something about the man unnerved him.

"I want a full report."

"The retrieval of the Raman Texts was successful. They have been transported to the hidden facility to be studied. Dr Omar has been..." Pulse paused to find the right word, "disposed of."

"Good," Jonas replied. "There's a new threat I want you to take care of."

"What threat?"

"Have you not read the papers? He's been all over the news."

"Sorry, sir, but I've been busy in Egypt."

Jonas was convinced that he caught a quick glimpse of a smirk on the scarred face of his henchman. Was it insolence? Choosing to ignore it, he remembered his father's lesson. He returned a smile.

"Zygonia has a new hero. Deal with him."

Before Pulse could answer, Jonas switched off the console. Pleased with his show of superiority, he sat back in his chair. Soon, he thought, there would be nothing left to stop him. Everything would be his.

He leant forward and pressed the red intercom button. "Monica, cancel my two o'clock meeting with the board. I have more important business to attend to."

**

Voltage sat on top of the tallest building overlooking the city. Cars hummed and honked as the late-night traffic began to build up. Zygonia was one of those places that never seemed to sleep; there was always traffic and people milling about in the maze of streets and avenues that crisscrossed the city like a complex Sudoku grid. The sky, however, seemed at peace. Not a cloud formed to hide away the stars or the moon. They beamed down from their lofty resting place, shining bright in the dark, masked eyes that watched over the scene below with a vigilant glare.

A week had passed since his heroic rescue of the hostages. The papers were full of stories about a masked man that had burst onto the scene to save the day. Was it a human or an alien hailing from a distant planet? Hero or villain? Is it okay for citizens to take the law into their own hands? And the tabloids; did he have a girlfriend? The media were quick to jump on the vigilante bandwagon. Some even claimed that he was a menace to society and should hand himself in. He wasn't sure what excited him more, the notoriety or the fact that somehow he had become a hero overnight. Everything was different now because of one quick-fire decision. He had a higher purpose. It felt as though he had become two different people; his normal, everyday self that went to school and lived a boring life, and then there was the brave, mysterious man behind the mask that had amazing powers. Kellen knew which part of himself he liked the most. He had even started understanding his abilities more, thanks to the professor's guidance.

Professor Drake had been the one to design Kellen's new uniform. The deep blue lightning insignia streaked across his chest like a beacon on its black leather background, all shiny and new. The suit was designed to help Kellen absorb and store as much electricity as he could to avoid 'burn out', as the professor called it. Not only that, but the head mask had two horn-shaped antenna, which would boost his ability to pick up any radio or digital frequencies floating through the air. That meant he could hear radio waves and tap into phone lines much easier now. It included listening in on the police broadband, but it also gave him a means of contacting the professor if he should get into any trouble. The final pieces of the jigsaw were his rubber-soled boots, which stopped him being 'earthed' and losing some of his potency; reinforced

Kevlar plates, which made it heavier but protected him from everything except a straight shot; and his gloves with their metal conductors attached to the palms, allowing him to focus energy for offensive purposes, even if they were only small lightning bolts at the moment.

The whole package was an indication of his arrival at hero status. The job of being a hero was a cinch; all week he had been on patrol without any problems. Nobody could stop him now, not all the time he was amped up. The geeky science nerd was long gone. Voltage was strong, confident and far surer of himself. Kellen chuckled. It was awesome being a god among men, he mused, shifting his position on the ledge next to the gargoyle he'd dubbed 'Bernie'.

His new uniform and career choices weren't the only changes that had taken place during the course of a week. It had also been a week since his first kiss with Linzi.

The memory of it had stuck in his mind the entire time; it was more important to him than all of the media attention put together. The first time he saw her, he had dreamed of the moment. Now it had become a reality, his emotions and feelings had skyrocketed. It had been everything he had expected and more, but the reality also brought with it doubts. There was no doubting she had enjoyed the moment as much as him; the bio-electric aura she gave off had almost blinded him. But the moment was with Voltage, not Kellen, and it was hard seeing her in class as if nothing between them had happened. He had desperately wanted to tell her the truth, but something inside him said he shouldn't. In a way, it was all awesome, but it was also a huge responsibility for him to take on. It was going to be a daunting task to resist not telling her and acting normal. He was a hero, but heroes don't have time for girlfriends, he thought, looking down at his watch.

It was getting late in the evening and he had to get up early in the morning for class. Trying to maintain a 4.0 grade point average and being a superhero was beginning to take its toll, even after only a week. The professor certainly wasn't going to cut him any slack, not in class or in training. He enjoyed the thrill of being out on patrol, but it wasn't so much fun only getting four hours sleep a night. And that was if he was lucky. On deeper reflection, being a hero had its downside.

"Well, time to turn in. Nighty night, Bernie," he said.

Even though he was over the other side of the city, the run back to the school dorms would only take him a few seconds. It had been a quiet night – only a couple of attempted robberies. That meant his body still had a lot of energy stored – enough to get him home anyway. He focused his mind inward, feeling the raw power that gathered at the centre of his body. The familiar tingle began spreading throughout his limbs, causing minimal vibrations.

His eyes flashed open with sparks. *Booom!*

Blue flashes of light sparked out beneath his feet as he zoomed down the wall of the building and along the road, zipping in and out between the cars. Bright coloured lights blended into one, giving off the illusion that he was running down a long tunnel. The wind rushed into his face, making his eyes water. He didn't care. Every time he ran, it felt as exhilarating as the first time. The only difference now was that he had more control and he knew how to start and stop under his own free will.

Learning how to use his powers was vital if he was to make the city a safer place. Fighting against criminals wasn't as easy as it looked on TV, and Kellen wasn't the most athletic of guys so he needed all the help he could get. It was handy having Professor Drake around to teach him how to use his powers more effectively; he was an expert at science and understood the transformation far better than anyone else. Kellen would be lost without him.

"Ahh! Help me, someone, please."

What the hell was that? He slammed on the brakes, dodging a bright yellow taxi as he did so. Late-night revellers stopped and stared in awe at the strange sight that had appeared out of nowhere in front of them. Kellen just ignored them, straining his ears to hear where the sound had come from.

"Please, someone."

That time he caught the sound. It was coming from one of the many dark alleyways that streaked off the main avenue. This time of night they harboured all kinds of crazy he was becoming accustomed to.

Damn it, he thought. It looked as though it was going to be a long night after all. Then again, he was the fastest man alive, so it wouldn't take more than a few seconds to wrap up some would-be muggers and alert police to pick them up. Time to crank it up, he thought, whizzing off in the direction of the screams.

Within seconds he was in the alleyway where he'd heard the sound. Dark shadows fell across his features as he slowly walked deeper into the confined space. Huge industrial dustbins overflowed with all kinds of muck, some of which

Kellen stepped in, not even wanting to know what it was. There was no sign of anyone in trouble. Nearby, a drainpipe dripped its contents across the alleyway. He stepped around the puddle to avoid the water.

"Help me!"

That was it. He shot off around the bend, deeper into the cavernous alleyway. In front of him was a single man bent over double, his back to Kellen.

"Sir, can I help you?" he asked, walking over and putting a hand on the man's shoulder.

Even with his newfound powers, he wasn't quick enough. A huge fist slammed into his jaw, sending him spinning through the air only to land with a dull thud against one of the dustbins. He heard several footsteps approaching.

"Well, well, boys. Look at what we have here. You hero types are all the same. One little scream and you can't resist coming to show off."

Kellen forced himself to rise on his elbows. The sudden punch had shocked him. Through the haze of pain, he could make out three figures. Each one of them masked by some kind of helmet.

"The boss is gonna love us," one of them said.

""Yeah, Mr Jonas is going to pay us a pretty penny for catching this little fish, Ramirez," the one who had been doubled over replied.

Jonas? It couldn't be the same Mr Jonas from the banquet? Why would he want me? Kellen wondered, snapping himself awake and standing to his feet. He was still dazed, but he took the best fighting stance he could muster.

"Don't you boys look all pretty, dolled up in your bright shiny uniforms," he said. Most thugs he came across on patrol so far were a mess, but these guys were different.

"Look, Zack, this one still wants to fight," the one known as Ramirez said in his high-pitched, Latino accent.

"I wanna pound on him," came a gruff voice from Kellen's left.

"Be my guest, Stacks."

The huge bear of a man came charging in. A black, gloved fist missed his head by a millimetre as he ducked under, jamming his own fist into Stacks' ribs.

"Ha-ha, you're no stronger than a fly."

"Actually, more like a bee."

Kellen focused a small taser-like charge into his palm and thrust upwards. It sent his opponent reeling backwards, but it wasn't enough to stop him.

"That tickled," Stacks said, charging again to grab with a vice-like bear hug.

This was it. Kellen whizzed around behind him, tapped him on the shoulder and threw the hardest punch he could manage. His knuckles crumpled under the impact, but he had managed to shatter the guy's helmet. Still, Stacks remained on his feet. Not wasting a second, Kellen ran six foot up the wall, spun off, slamming another punch into the exposed face of his aggressor.

Super-speed time.

Blow after blow rained down on Stacks. After a few seconds, he stood there, swaying left to right on his feet.

"Had enough yet, big boy?" Kellen asked, still swaying himself.

"I'm gonna crush you!" Stacks screamed.

Too slow. In the blink of an eye, Kellen sidestepped, thrusting out his arm to send a small shock through Stacks' body, who landed in a steaming heap on the floor. He was out cold.

Kellen turned to the other two. "You two want to dance as well?"

The two of them stood there for a second, mouths agape, staring at their huge comrade unconscious on the floor.

"Let's take him down together, Ramirez."

The one called Zack circled to Kellen's left, while Ramirez circled to his right holding a knife.

"Divide and conquer, fellas? You do know that I'm fast, right?"

In one quick blur of motion, the fight was over. First, he sent a small shock in the direction of Ramirez, stunning him long enough for Kellen to shoot to his left, taking out Zack with a couple of quick fire punches, before going back to the right, finishing off by zapping the last of the trio, putting him to bed. They didn't stand a chance, Kellen thought, as he started tying them up with the rope he held in his belt.

He could feel that the energy in his body was running low. The big guy had really taken his toll. Now Kellen would have to walk home.

He hadn't quite learnt how to generate his own electricity yet and he wasn't keen on absorbing more from the surrounding buildings, as Professor Drake said that might be dangerous. He wasn't even sure he had enough juice to notify the police on their scanners so that they could come and pick up the three goons, now safely tied up at his feet. If there was a police car nearby it wouldn't cost him too much. He closed his eyes and pushed out his senses.

"Bravo, young man. You've done well to beat my Hell Raisers."

The deep voice from above snapped him back. Now what? he thought, turning around to face the person that had addressed him.

"Look, dude, I—"

Kellen cut the sentence short. Perched above him was the most sinister man he had ever seen, glaring down at him with a single eye, the other hidden behind a black eye-patch.

"I take it you want these guys back? Well, Pops, save yourself the trouble. By the time they wake up, they'll be tucked away behind bars." He could take this guy, he thought, even with only a small amount of power left.

Pulse drew a faint smile across his lips. Such insolence in the young these days, he mused. He would teach him how to respect his elders.

Slowly, he raised his arm, holding out his palm. Voltage just stood there, arms crossed in front of his new emblem. With a quick shove of his hand, Pulse sent the would-be hero slamming against a brick wall.

Kellen's head smashed against the wall, almost knocking him unconscious. What the hell was that? He managed to push himself up onto his knees, only to be hurtled sideways into a pile of trash.

Leaping off of the fire escape, Pulse landed in a crouch, hopped into a somersault and then he was standing, laughing at the poor wreck moaning in the pile of black bags. He was only just warming up.

"You may think you're powerful, boy, but there are those out there far more dangerous than you."

"Thanks for the info, Pops," Kellen retorted, managing to hurl a lightning bolt in the direction of his attacker.

Pulse merely batted the lightning bolt aside with his telekinetic abilities, as if it was nothing but a fly. "Your little tricks won't work on me. But mine will work on you!"

Kellen felt himself being lifted into the air by invisible hands. The pressure tightened around his chest, cracking his ribs and constricting his breathing. He had to think of something fast. Maybe if he could get close enough?

"Ahh, please."

"Ha-ha, a hero begging for mercy. I've seen it all now," Pulse said, flinging Kellen's battered body across the alleyway. "God knows why anyone would consider you to be an obstacle. You're pathetic."

With broken ribs and very little reserve left, Kellen refused to let this nutcase win. He managed to get to his feet, his head pounding, as if a marching band was on parade in his skull. A small mouthful of blood erupted on him, splattering down his new uniform. He had one shot to pull this off.

"Is that the best you've got, Pops? There was me thinking you'd be a challenge."

Pulse laughed. "You've got spunk, kid. I like that. Pity I have to kill you really. You would've made a good pupil."

The few seconds of banter were all Kellen needed. He managed to draw a small amount of energy from the nearby building that he had been thrown against. The silver-haired guy in front of him had foolishly stepped into the puddle from the leaking drainpipe.

"Yo, Pops, science lesson number one. Never mix electricity with water!"

He slammed his hand down into the long winding puddle, sending brilliant blue streaks of lightning hurtling along the floor and up his attacker's body. The electricity forked all around them as Kellen gave it all he had; it was almost as if he was enjoying the rush. The scream from the old guy pierced through him.

He stopped, disgusted with himself. He had almost killed the guy, who was now lying face down in the water. A few more seconds and whoever he was would have been toast. It would have been so easy with his powers to have crossed the line from hero to villain; the two were that close.

He spun around, hearing running footsteps and shouts coming towards him. All the commotion must have alerted the police, he thought. With some areas of the media screaming for his arrest, he couldn't afford to be seen by them until he had proved he was a on their side. Although, he wasn't sure after tonight that he *was* a hero. He didn't feel like one any more.

Despite the small amount of electricity he had gathered, he could feel his body failing fast. He felt the familiar vibrating and then shot off up the side of the building, landing on the roof. In a few seconds he would pass out. He felt through the hundreds of different radio frequencies filtering through the sky, looking for ones he could latch on to.

There was the one he was looking for.

"Professor Drake, help me."

He collapsed.

Down below the police rounded up three unconscious bodies. A fourth hid in the shadows, vowing to get his revenge.

***

On the other side of town, in the shadow of a Romanesque column, Agent Victoria Enhardt smoked the last dregs of her cigarette before stamping it out with her high-heeled shoes. At this time of night, this was the last place she wanted to be, waiting for her partner to show up, late as usual. She put her hands in the pockets of her long brown jacket to keep them warm. It was getting cold, she thought, as she noticed the steam from her breath rising in front of her face. All she could think about was being home, tucked up in a nice warm bed with a tub of B&J.

She hadn't really wanted the case; it would probably just turn out to be a simple robbery. It was more for her career that she had taken it. Something about this one seemed unusual and if she could work it out then maybe she would finally get the promotion she had been working towards.

She took a quick glance down the street. Police officers were milling around outside the station, filing in and out of the old building. A car with blaring music sped down the road, catching her attention. It halted at the side of the kerb with a screech from the tyres. She couldn't see through the black tinted windows, but she knew who it was.

"Hey, Vicky, what's up?" The suited man said, as he stepped out of the black sedan.

"Agent Montella, nice of you to drop by," Victoria replied. They'd been partners for a long time and he knew just how to infuriate her.

"Please, Vicky, why so formal? You remember that night in Cobalt City, right? Call me Vinnie."

"Just get over here will you. We've got work to do."

"I'm yours to command. Lead the way, ma'am."

Victoria rolled her eyes and walked up the steps.

Chapter Nine

Victoria went first as the two entered through the rotating door. Despite the constant flow of the officers in and out of the building, the lobby seemed to be pretty quiet; the odd drunk and perpetrator waiting to be processed was all the business they seemed to be doing. She walked straight up to the grizzled old sergeant at the front desk, flashing her badge and introducing herself and her partner. The sergeant barely took any notice, pressed the button behind the desk and buzzed them through. The two agents went around the side of the desk and through the back door. As they did so, another officer in a beige suit and tie came rushing towards them, his shining brown shoes tap-tapping on the linoleum floor.

"Agents, I—I—I didn't expect the feds to send anyone down here this late. Can I help you? I'm Detective Todd."

"Evening, Detective, we're here to question one of your suspects from the museum robbery. I believe his name's…" Victoria stopped to check her data-pad. Vinnie just stood behind her, looking bored as always. "Ah, here we go. His name's Tad Dillan."

"Oh yes, I know who you mean. Strange one, that one. He was the only one out of the bunch that survived. Reckons they were set up. Me and my boys haven't found any evidence to suggest it though. If you ask me, it's all the drugs and violent TV that kids watch these days. Makes 'em crazy."

"Thanks for the assessment," Vinnie said with a snort.

Victoria gave him a quick elbow in the ribs to shut him up.

"So you think it was just a simple robbery that went wrong?" she asked.

"Like I said, there's no evidence to suggest anything else."

"I'd like to speak to the kid myself. Can you show us where he is?"

"You'll be wasting your time, but yeah, I can take you up to the interview rooms. Haven't had much to do around here since that new guy came on the scene. This way."

Before Victoria could ask him what he meant by the new guy, he was ushering them along the corridor and into a lift. She hesitated before getting in.

"Are there any stairs?" she asked, feeling her heartbeat quicken.

"Uh, yeah, they're down the end of the hallway, then take a left. You should see 'em right in front of you. I'll have the kid sent up."

"Thank you," she said, then turning to Vinnie. "You take the lift, I'll take the stairs."

Vinnie just laughed and pressed the button to close the doors. At times he was a real clown, but over the years she had learnt to ignore his weird sense of humour. They had become quite close friends and deep down she knew he wouldn't let anything happen to her.

She made her way in the direction the detective had shown her. This was probably one of the quietest precincts she had ever been in. She looked down at her watch. It was only twelve thirty a.m. according to the green digital display. Police stations were usually buzzing with activity this time of night, full of drunks and gang members. But this one seemed more like a morgue. Even the officers on duty were half-asleep, roving around the corridors like zombies. In one office she passed, several of the officers were playing a game of cards. Something at the back of her mind was nagging at her. There was a reason why there was a lack of activity, but she just couldn't put her finger on it. Like a child grasping for the cookie jar, her mind just couldn't reach the thoughts. It was something she had read in the paper. No doubt it would come back to her later, she thought, as she climbed the long winding staircase to the fifth floor.

By the time she reached her destination, she was panting. Vinnie was already waiting for her, lounging against the wall. His arms were folded across his chest, bouncing up and down as he chuckled away to himself. She fixed him the most hateful stare she could muster.

"You're an ass. Why can't you be serious for once, huh?"

"Not in my nature, sweetheart. But I do love it when you give me the sexy eye."

She sighed and just walked off in the direction of another desk sergeant. Vinnie was a goofball and always would be; she didn't know why she kept trying to change him. The desk sergeant just continued reading his magazine, oblivious to the two federal agents. Victoria cleared her throat.

"What?"

"We need an interview room," she replied to the rude man. What was wrong with this station?

"Down on the right, room sixteen."

Without even bothering to thank the sergeant, she walked off to find the room with her partner. The sooner they were out of this place the better. It was no wonder Zygonia had such a high crime rate if this was how the police departments operated.

Vinnie tapped her on the shoulder. "Why have we been put on this case? The bureau doesn't deal with simple theft, especially not our division."

"Agent Montella, I take it you didn't read the briefing?"

He just shrugged. "I had a hot date."

"Agents don't have time for dating," she informed him, entering the room.

She groped around the cold wall with her hand, searching for the light switch. She found it. Her eyes blinked a few times as the bright yellow light dazzled her. It was no different from any other interview room she had been in; its dull battleship-grey walls, white tiled floor and single florescent light the only decorations. Along one wall was the typical dark, two-way mirror. There were no windows to let in fresh air. She took a deep breath as she closed the door behind her colleague; her palms already felt damp.

"This is no ordinary heist," she continued. "The item in question is of interest to our superiors. Also, according to the security cameras, all the men that were found locked inside were the only ones that entered. All dead, except one witness."

"Oh right, so you're thinking something unnatural?"

"Well the staff didn't steal itself."

"Guess not. Doubt this kid'll have the answers though. Surely the detectives would've chased up any leads?"

"This police force?" Victoria said, raising her eyebrows. The district attorney's office had become very good at hiding the city's true crime figures. "I doubt it. We're on our own for this one. The bureau wants answers."

"Well, I want coffee. Do you want some?"

"Please," she replied.

Vinnie left the room, closing the door behind him. It was silent except for the constant humming from the tube of light above her head. She sat down on one of the hard black chairs behind a metal table that comprised the only furniture in the room. Her hands were shaking and her breath was beginning to quicken. She rubbed her temples to relax. The door handle clicked as Vinnie returned with the steaming hot cups. "They're just bringing him now," he informed her.

"Okay."

It was time for answers.

***

"Mr Dillan, I'm Agent Victoria Enhardt of the FBI. Is it okay to go over some questions?"

"I guess so," Tad replied, his eyes fixed at a spot on the table.

Victoria sat upright on her seat. She continued to watch the young man sitting opposite her. Body language meant everything in this game. He certainly didn't look like the typical criminal. His head was bowed and his shoulders slumped forward, his jade-green eyes looked haunted. Something was amiss.

"What were you doing in the museum on the night of the sixteenth?" she asked, taking a soft approach.

The kid looked terrified. "I told you guys already. I wasn't there to steal anything. It's my mum; we can't afford to pay for her medicine, what with me being at school and all. I just wanted to help out."

Tears welled in his eyes, a single drop splashed on to the cold table top.

Victoria let him wipe his eyes before continuing. "You were found with three dead bodies, all with criminal records, and two dead guards." The mention of the guards made him fidget. "You were the only people to enter that building. Did you kill them?"

"No!" Tad shouted, looking up for the first time. "I was just there to open the security locks inside. Jacob said it would be easy. Straight in, straight out. It was only a dumb stick. Now they're dead. I—I never killed nobody, ma'am, honest I didn't."

"Then what the hell happened in there?"

"It was that guy, the one with the silver hair and the scar. H—He set us up."

Now they were getting somewhere, information she could use. "A man with a scar?"

"Y—Y—Yeah he was real scary. He killed the guards and attacked us." Tad shook as the words tumbled from his mouth.

Victoria couldn't work out if he was telling the truth or not. She needed more information on this mysterious man he claimed had set them up. Taking a sip of her, now cold, coffee, her steel gaze bore in to him over the rim of the cup. Everything about his body language screamed he was telling the truth. There was something she was missing.

"According to the security data, you four were the only ones inside except the guards. There was no one else."

"He was there!" Tad screamed.

She could tell he was getting agitated. "You're lying."

"I swear he was there. Please, you gotta believe me."

"How could one man take on four armed men?"

"I told you guys already, I don't know how he did it. One minute I was standing there, then I was flung across the room like a piece of trash. It was weird. It felt like a wall had hit me, leaving me all tingling like static off a balloon. It was as if he had magical powers, or something."

That was it; her mind finally grasped the cookie jar. All week she had read in the news about a vigilante they had dubbed 'Voltage'. He was supposed to be some kind of superhero with special abilities. Maybe the hero act was exactly that, nothing more than a simple ruse to cover up his more nefarious nature? She was convinced it had to be him; how many more freaks with powers could there be in Zygonia City?

"Thank you for your cooperation," she said, almost knocking over the remainder of the polystyrene cup sitting on the table as she darted for the door.

"Do I get to go home now?" Tad asked.

She smiled at him. "I'm sorry, but no."

***

Victoria had rounded up every single officer she could find and crammed them all into one tiny office. Most of them had moaned at her for calling them in. She didn't care as it was about time that they earned their pay. Vinnie had also protested, claiming the kid had got it wrong. Nothing would stop her from taking the vigilante down; the more she thought about it, the more certain she was that he had to be stopped. If she managed to pull it off, she would have secured her promotion and would be leading her division, rather than being stuck in a grotty police station in the middle of the night.

She surveyed the crowd in front of her, most of whom were half-asleep or chatting away to each other about the Zappers recent success in the cup. She banged her hand down hard on the table to get their attention. They completely ignored her, except one, who jumped out of his seat, spilling coffee all over himself. Vinnie put his hand on her shoulder.

"Yo, people, can we get some quiet please?" he asked the crowd, immediately gaining their attention.

Victoria looked at him with daggers in her eyes. "Thank you, Agent Montella," she said through gritted teeth. "I want every single officer here to listen carefully. This new vigilante parading around like a hero needs to be stopped at once."

"But why?" a female officer asked. "He's cleaning up the streets. In a week, he's done what we've been trying to do for years."

"Yeah, why would we want to stop him and make more work for ourselves?" a male officer chimed in, to a chorus of laughter.

Victoria had already known she was going to have problems with this bunch.

"That may be, but new evidence suggests he is a danger to society and must be stopped. If you're not willing to follow my lead, I can always go back to my superiors and inform them of this station's inactivity. The mayor is always eager to save public funds." That would get their attention, she thought, with a smug smile.

Vinnie stepped forward. "What my colleague here is trying to say is that you guys could earn yourselves a reputation as the best, *if* you can pull this off."

"We are the best," another officer shouted.

"Indeed you are. Now what we want is an APB put out on this guy. Unless you want this amateur stealing all your thunder?"

The crowd erupted with a chorus of 'no ways'. Victoria was glaring at him. She was the one that was supposed to be in charge, not him. How could this goofball get everyone's respect when all he ever did was fool around? She tried to ignore her jealousy. He had their attention and so it didn't really matter, she told herself.

Vinnie continued. "We want every available officer searching the streets for him. He has to be out there somewhere, so come on, guys, let's find him and make the streets safe."

The room erupted into activity. Officers flitted to and fro in their haste to get the job done.

After a few minutes, the two agents were left alone in the room. Victoria was picking up all of her papers off the desk. In a way, she admired the way her partner handled situations; he had a way with people that endeared them to him. It was something she had never been able to do. Maybe she would learn one day.

Vinnie cleared the back of his throat to get her attention. "How did I do, boss?"

"You did good."

"Wow, praise off the famous Agent Enhardt. I must be doing something right."

"Don't get too cocky, we've still got a criminal to catch. A highly dangerous one at that."

"Do you really think he did it?"

"Who else do you know of that has special powers? It has to be him. If not, our division is going to be pretty busy from now on. After all, we were set up to prevent things like this."

Doubts were starting to creep in to her mind now, but she pushed them to the back. All she ever wanted was a career in law enforcement and this bust could really push her up the food chain. If anyone else knew of her doubts, it could cause all manner of problems for the investigation. She had to have a granite resolve if she was to pull this off.

"Well, it's getting late and I need to get some sleep. We can't do anything tonight. Maybe you should think about getting home too?" Vinnie said, edging towards the door. "I can give you a ride."

"No, thank you. I'm going to hang around here for a while and look through some of the paperwork on this guy."

"Okay then, just promise me something? If you find him, don't try and do this alone. If you're right about him then it could be dangerous."

"I'll be fine. You go home and get some rest. I'll see you in the morning."

After that Vinnie left, leaving Victoria alone in the bright room sifting through papers. If she wanted her promotion, then she had to get cracking with the job. She couldn't afford to sleep, she thought, as she looked out of the window into the dark night. He was out there somewhere. And it was up to her to find him.

Chapter Ten

Kellen woke up for the second time that week in strange surroundings. The sunlight streaked through the crack in the curtains, bathing the white bed covers in a clean golden swathe. He blinked to clear the hazy vision left by a deep sleep, realising he was on a moth-eaten couch back in the professor's office. The familiar sight of academic papers and textbooks piled high warmed him. The glowing blue static electricity ball had been removed this time; the professor clearly thought it would be too much of a temptation.

As he went to move, extreme pain shot through his body as if he was a boil being lanced. Memories from last night's encounter came flooding back to him with an overwhelming sense of failure. He had been either too dumb or too arrogant with his powers. Either way, the bluish-green bruises speckling his body were testament to the fact that from now on he would be taking his abilities far more seriously.

Managing to pull himself out of bed, his battered body moaned with the exertion of moving towards the window. Somewhere out there, he thought, was his scarred attacker and his merry band. Who the hell was he? The thought made him shudder; he hadn't stood a chance against the more experienced man. It wasn't the powers he was worried about, although they did come as a shock; it was the mention of Mr Jonas that had unsettled him. Why did Jonas want Voltage? Jonas was just a businessman and philanthropist.

All the questions buzzed around Kellen's mind like hornets in a nest, making his head throb more than it already did, but he couldn't ignore the problem. The silver-haired maniac obviously had connections to Mr Jonas, but Kellen had no idea what they were.

"Professor Drake, you here?" he called out.

There was no answer. He had to find out more about Jonas, but there was no way he could take on his new nemesis until his body healed. Sending out his senses, he searched for the familiar signature of the telephone line. After a few seconds he latched on to it, mentally dialling the number he wanted.

"Howdy-ho," the faint voice said on the other end.

"Dan, it's me, Kellen."

"Yo, buddy, what can I do for you?"

"I need a hand with some research in the library if you're up for it?"

"Well, let me check my diary." Dan paused, leaving Kellen straining to hold on to the thin connection. His head felt like the football team marching band were practicing in there again.

"Yeah, I'll see you there in thirty," Dan finally said.

Kellen let the connection go, sweating. After throwing on the clothes that the professor had kindly picked up for him and left on the side, he darted out of the door. There was no time to lose. He had to find out more.

***

Kellen shot over the quad as fast as his feet could carry him without using his powers. He dodged footballs and Frisbees flying through the warm March air as throngs of people enjoyed the brilliant sunshine. There were far too many for him to even think about super-speeding over to the school library; there was every chance that he would get caught, which would mean game over. It wasn't far from the professor's office to the library, but the time he spent walking was time wasted.

When he arrived, Dan was already standing outside the tall glass building munching on a hotdog. He waved at his friend as he approached. They greeted each other as friends do, using their own customary handshake. Kellen was glad he wouldn't have to do this alone.

"We gonna stand out here all day?" Dan said, his usual happy self. "They got air conditioning in there."

The bad mood that had developed as Kellen made his way over evaporated. He could always count on Dan to cheer him up, he realised.

"Yo, look who it is," a voice said as they were about to leave. "The fat boy and the geek."

Kellen watched Zach Lietzke strut up to them, flanked by his heavies.

Zach was the local bully with a penchant for tormenting his victims. And it just so happened that he'd been gunning for Kellen and Dan since the beginning of the year, despite the fact that they'd done nothing to deserve it.

Kellen felt Dan back away a step. Kellen just stood his ground. He didn't have time for this.

"Get lost, Zach."

"What's this? Has the nerd finally grown a spine?"

"I said back off."

"Make me, princess."

The two boys squared off against each other. Kellen felt a tug at his arm.

"Come on," Dan whispered. "Let's just get out of here."

"Yeah, listen to your boyfriend."

Kellen shoved the bigger boy backwards. It would be so easy to fry him right there on the spot, he thought, sparks darting around his eyes.

No, he realised, he couldn't do that. But there was one thing he could do.

Zach came forward again, shoving Kellen in the chest. As he did, Kellen allowed a small static shock to pass through him, acting like a taser.

"Jesus, what the hell?" he shouted.

Kellen just smiled.

Zach looked confused, eyes darting from one boy to the other. He brushed himself off. "Don't ever let me catch you two out here again or you'll be toast."

With those parting words, he left with his friends. Dan put his hand on Kellen's shoulder.

"Well that was a close one," he said with a sigh of relief. "What the hell's got in to you?"

"Let's just say, I'm not going to be intimidated by bullies like Zach Lietzke any more," Kellen replied. "Come on, let's get going. We've wasted enough time already."

Inside the library, they made their way to the computer suite on the top floor. The entire building was surrounded by huge glass windows that reflected during the day but allowed curious eyes to look in after dark. It featured a small drinks kiosk; two garden terraces, one with views over the city; and an atrium. The long, winding staircase coiled its way upwards like a snake in the centre of the lobby. Students dashed to and fro across wide bridges connecting the never-ending lines of dusty books, hurrying to meet their deadlines. There was hardly ever anyone up top, which is what Kellen wanted, little or no distraction. He had work of his own to do. Fast.

Dan tapped him on the shoulder. "Umm, what're we doing here?"

"We need to find as much information as we can on JonasTech. Newspaper clippings, magazine articles, websites: that kind of stuff."

"Oh right," Dan replied, scratching his head. "This might be a dumb question, but why?"

Kellen had to think quickly on his feet. He couldn't exactly tell his friend that they were searching for links to a possible super villain.

"I'm thinking of taking that internship I was offered at the banquet," he lied to his friend. "I want to know more about my potential employers."

He hated doing it but there was no other choice. A part of him wanted to tell Dan the truth about the changes in his life. They had been friends for a long time, but he couldn't take the chance of having his secret exposed. Not only that, if Dan knew, it might put him, like Linzi, in danger. It was just another one of the ever-growing burdens he had to bear since becoming a hero.

The two of them decided it would be best to split the workload between them; Dan would take care of newspapers and magazines, Kellen would cover trawling through the millions of websites that had pieces on Mr Jonas and his company. He sighed deeply. They would be here forever, he thought, staring at the flickering screen. Without wasting any more time, he cracked on with his investigation.

***

After two hours, he was beginning to give up hope. There was nothing incriminating he could find. JonasTech seemed to be a legitimate business that made huge profits every year, all of which was above board. They had made huge advances in most areas of science and innovation, and Mr Jonas even made annual donations to over twenty charities. It was hopeless.

Kellen threw his pen across the room in frustration, narrowly missing a fellow student bent over a desk. The girl looked up to see where the pen had come from, shooting daggers in Kellen's direction. He just slumped down in his seat, face burning, as it turned bright red. It was unlike him to lose his temper. The need to find out information was bordering on obsession. It was time for a break.

Leaving the computer screen glaring behind him, he went down to the basement rooms that housed the millions of old magazines and newspaper holograms in search of Dan. He hoped his friend had found something useful. It took him a while to find him.

"Found anything?" he asked, not wanting to sound too desperate.

"I'm not really sure what I'm supposed to be looking for."

"Have you found anything…" he paused in search of the right word to use, "unsavoury on the company?"

Dan shifted around his pieces of paper. Kellen held his breath, not even wanting to blink. "There was this. It's pretty recent."

"How recent?"

"Like a week ago, just over," Dan said, passing Kellen the notes he had made from the holograms.

Kellen read them. It was an article about a robbery that had taken place at the National Museum. He gave his forehead a loud slap. Of course, that was it, he thought, starting to dash off back towards the entrance of the library. Mr Jonas owned the museum that had been the scene of the crime; a crime which the media claimed was unexplainable. No item could steal itself, but Kellen knew somebody that could get in and out with it.

Cogs turned in his head as he mulled over whether this was a strong enough piece of evidence to connect Jonas with the silver-haired attacker. Part of him reasoned it wasn't; just because the crime was unexplainable and Mr Jonas owned the place, it didn't mean it was an inside job. On the other hand, it was all he had to go on.

"Hey, where are you going now?" Dan called from behind him. Kellen had forgotten his friend had been the one to find the information. He turned back.

"Thanks, Dan, this is exactly what I needed."

"No problemo, amigo. Let's go and celebrate?"

"I'd love to, but I can't," Kellen explained, watching his friend's smile drop down to a frown. He couldn't afford for Dan to get suspicious. "I'm not feeling too good. All that staring at a screen has given me a headache. I think I'll just go home and have a lie down."

"Okay then, I'll give you a call later."

"Yeah, that would be great. See you tomorrow."

Within the next minute or two he was outside in the fresh air. A new resolve had rooted itself deep inside him. There was a constant fear that he would go over to the museum and find nothing. But there was also a chance he might find the answers he needed.

Something inside him, some ill omen, was growing. It was telling him that danger was lurking just around the corner if he didn't find the answers. And in some way, the museum robbery was the key to it all.

***

Night had fallen over the city long after Kellen had decided to follow his lead, but someone else was also following a lead of their own.

Victoria rushed through the streets of Zygonia like a demon. It was the only sure sighting of the masked hero for over twenty-four hours. She was now in charge of apprehending Voltage and this may be her only chance, she thought, tyres screeching as she rounded the corner.

Vinnie had insisted that she contact him if there were any sightings; he reckoned it would be dangerous for her to try and tackle him alone. But as usual, she had gone off without any backup. It would be her bust and no one else's.

Looking at her watch, her foot slammed down hard on the accelerator, tall buildings screamed past her in a blur as the car flew down the road towards the museum. By all accounts, Voltage was extremely fast. For all she knew he could be gone by now. There was very little time to spare.

The Zygonia National Museum loomed large, casting long shadows over her as she pulled the car up outside the front entrance. Nothing stirred. He had to be there, she thought, closing the car door and quietly making her way up the long white steps, her eyes darting over the building, looking for any sign of him. The windows remained cold and dark. There was no sign of anything, let alone a thief. Catching Voltage by surprise would be the key. There was no way that she would be able to do it if he knew she was coming; he was far too sly. Remembering Vinnie's words, she drew her gun as she peered through the tall double doors of the building.

Nobody had set foot inside the museum since the robbery. The lobby remained dead. She could see dust gathering on the stone statues of past presidents. The huge portraits on the wall stared solemnly in to the empty room. The long faces had an air of sadness about them. It was as if the building was dying from lack of love and attention. Places like this needed people to visit or they fell in to decay. The thought of going into the empty building that usually heaved with curious bodies made Victoria shiver. At least the halls and corridors were ginormous caverns, she joked, trying to cover up her own growing nervousness. She pulled at the door.

It was locked tight. She pulled again and again, but the door just rattled in its frame. It wouldn't do to smash the glass in case he was inside. She swore to the night sky under her breath. How was she going to get inside now? Every second she wasted was another second for Voltage to get away. There had to be a way in.

She quickly ran around the building searching for an open window, an air vent, any opening she could crawl through. But there was nothing. The forensic guys had done a good job sealing up the crime scene. Her last hope was the rear entrance, which was used for deliveries and moving exhibits to and from the building. To her knowledge, it had an electric security lock that required a code. Maybe she could hack in to it. There was nothing to lose by trying, she told herself, as she made her way around to the rear of the building.

When she saw the door, her heart skipped a beat. It was ajar, the lock spitting sparks and smoke in to the night sky.

She drew her gun for a second time and made her way into the building. Moving left and right through the long storage aisles, her breath came in rapid bursts. Over and over again she told herself he had to be here, passing row upon row of exhibits covered with long white sheets that looked like ghosts in the gloom.

After the storage room, she entered one of the main corridors. Still nothing stirred. The only sound was from her heels on the marble floor, which she rapidly took off, her gun pointing forward, as she walked towards the Egyptian display. Part of her wanted to call for backup but her pride wouldn't let her. It was hard enough for women at the bureau to gain the respect of the men and she had worked damn hard to get up the ladder. There was no way she was going to throw it all away because of a few shadows making her nervous. She was trained for this. Her whole career was based on the threat of possible superhuman anomalies. A new steel hard determination lent speed to her step. He wouldn't get away again.

There was a loud clang from the room at the end of the corridor.

"Oops," a voice muttered. "Hope it wasn't expensive."

It was coming from the Egyptian display. If it was Voltage, he wasn't a stealthy thief. A sudden thought occurred to her. Why would he come back to the scene of his crime? It went against everything she had learnt at the academy. It wasn't as if there was anything to cover up; the police had taken all of the evidence they could find. Maybe he was just greedy? But then if that was the case, he would have taken everything the first time around, not done it in two trips.

She pushed the thoughts from her mind. It was him, she knew it. She kept her back to the wall, gun close to her chest. This was it; her moment. She took a deep breath.

Quickly, she spun around the opening, pointing her gun straight at Voltage. Her eyes glimmered in the small shaft of moonlight that cut across her face. Their gazes locked. She had him now.

Chapter Eleven

"FBI, freeze!" Victoria shouted, pointing her gun at the masked man in front of her.

"Umm, this isn't what you think, lady," Kellen replied, not taking his eyes off the gun. He knew he was quick, but he wasn't sure if he was quick enough to dodge a speeding bullet. He hadn't even bothered to try in the jewellers.

"Don't move an inch, freak."

"Now that's just mean. There's no need to get personal."

"Oh great, another wise-guy. You're under arrest for the robbery of the Zygonia National Museum and five counts of murder."

"What?" Kellen said, his eyes wide with surprise. He moved a couple of steps towards her.

"Come any closer and I swear to God I'll shoot."

"I haven't done anything!"

"You can tell your story down at the police station."

"You gotta catch me first, lady."

Kellen whipped around the room to the thunderous applause of gunfire ricocheting off the walls, each shot echoing through the cavernous room. He knew if she carried on firing, it would alert any passers-by outside. This had to end fast.

"Yo, lady, stop firing. I'm on your side," he called out from behind a marble pillar.

"Like hell you are," Victoria replied, reloading her gun. "Your goody-two-shoes act doesn't fool me. We got a witness to prove that you're guilty."

Kellen had lost sight of where she was in his haste to dodge the bullets. To his left, along the wall, were tiny holes like pockmarks, where the gun had spat its deadly hail of bullets. That meant she was somewhere behind him. At least now I know I can dodge bullets, he thought, as he sent out his senses to pinpoint her location.

"I'm innocent. Your witness has it all wrong," he said, trying to stall her. His powers weren't quite up to scratch yet, so it still took him time to trigger each ability.

"Give it up, Voltage. You're coming with me, whichever way you choose to do this."

He really didn't want to have to hurt her, but if she carried on this way, then he would have no choice. "Look, lady, if you keep firing that thing at me, I'm going to have to get tough."

After a few more seconds, his extra senses locked onto the vibrant bio-electricity she was radiating. He built up the vibrations in his body. With a flash he was around behind her, snatching the gun and then returning to the centre of the room. A broad smile appeared on his lips.

Victoria just stood there dumbfounded. Kellen shot out a bolt of electricity, aiming for the security lock. The first missed, but the second zapped straight onto the target, frying the mechanism and sending the security door tumbling down to block off her passage. She turned to look at him like a deer caught in the headlights of a car. He needed to calm her down. Maybe they could work together.

"I told you, lady. I'm on your side."

"You don't frighten me. If you murder me, the entire bureau will be on you like a pack of wolves," Victoria said, standing firm with a defiant glint in her eye. "You won't be able to fart for fear of getting caught."

Kellen let out a small chuckle. "Well, I always wanted to be famous."

"You're nothing but a crook!"

"I'm no crook. I've been bustin' my butt off all week trying to help you guys clean up this town. Now you want to arrest me?"

"It has to be you," Victoria announced, her eyes darting around looking for an escape route. "How many other freaks do you know of with special abilities?"

That was it, the information he had been looking for to tie Jonas to the museum. The guy that had committed this robbery, the same crime that Kellen was now being accused of, had to be the same man that attacked him the night before. The thought of his mysterious attacker caused the pain from his battered body to throb again, as if the memory of it was just as painful as the event itself.

"Did you say a guy with powers?" he asked.

"Yeah, as far as I know you're the only freak around here."

"There you go again, getting personal. Well sorry to burst you're bubble, lady, but it's not me. I do know who it is though."

The last sentence made Victoria's eyes fall on him, her stance becoming more natural and relaxed. He had got her attention.

***

The moonlight shone through the lofty windows, bathing the room in its soft glow. The two of them stood, squaring off against each other with neither one of them conceding an inch. Kellen just stood in the centre of the room, his arms folded across his chest and an ever-present smile across his face. He had found a way to get her to listen to him, but Victoria still looked as though she was ready to put up a fight.

"What do you mean, you know who did it?" she asked, narrowing her eyes almost to a squint.

"I know the man you're looking for and it's not me. If you promise not to shoot at me, I'll give you your gun back."

"You're lying."

"Look, I could just as easily leave you here for the security guards to find you in the morning. But I want to help. We're looking for the same person."

"Okay," she said, mimicking his relaxed posture. "Talk."

Kellen explained the events of the previous night, hoping she would see that he was the good guy in all of this. He told her of how he had been attacked and was now looking for the man that did it. What he didn't tell her was the connection between that man and Mr Jonas. He didn't want to lay all of his cards on the table in case he couldn't trust her. There were stories of corruption in the police force all the time. How did he know she wasn't a dirty cop?

"How do I know you're not lying?" she asked.

"I don't know. You'll just have to trust me."

Victoria snorted her derision. "Like I haven't heard that one before. What does this mysterious man look like?"

He went in to great detail describing the sinister look of his assailant and how his most distinguishing feature was the scar that ran the length of his jaw. After he had finished telling her his story, she started to pace around the room, mulling over what he had told her. Kellen just stood there not really knowing what to do.

"Let's say you're telling me the truth. That means there are more like you in Zygonia?"

It was a question that he'd been mulling over in his head since his encounter. The day he had realised the changes in his body, he had thought he was unique in the world. It had made him feel special. The thought of there being more people like him out there dampened that feeling. On the one hand, it meant that others were going through the triumphs and pitfalls of having abilities just like him. But on the other, it depended on how those others were using their abilities. So far, the thought of meeting more people like him wasn't too appealing. The weight of having these powers sat heavily on his shoulders. More than ever, he realised the responsibility he had now – not only to himself, but to the entire world. It was a big task to take on at his age. First he had to stop whatever was going on in Zygonia.

"Yeah, I guess it does mean I'm not the only one."

Victoria still didn't look satisfied. "How do I know you haven't made this guy up?"

"You got to believe me. If we work together, maybe we can solve this mess?"

"Hmm, prove it. Take off your mask."

"No way!" Kellen exclaimed. There was no way he was going to reveal his true identity to her. She could be anyone. He was never going to put his family and friends in danger like that. "If you can't trust me, then I'm out of here."

He began building up the vibrations in his body, readying himself to set off.

"Wait!" Victoria shouted. "Maybe we should pool our resources." The sentence was more a statement than a question.

"Then I'm going to need everything you know."

***

The two of them sat down for an hour, exchanging information. Neither one of them completely trusted the other. They were still no closer to uncovering the truth. All they knew was that, somehow, JonasTech was involved.

"I never did like that guy," Victoria said.

"We don't know how involved he is yet. It could be blackmail, or extortion. Why would a rich guy need to steal a dumb stick?"

"Leave the investigating to the pros." Victoria got up to leave, picking up her gun on the way. "You just stay out of this and hang up that mask. The bureau doesn't like outsiders interfering. If I see you again, I'm going to use all the resources available to put you behind bars."

"And there was me thinking we was getting along," Kellen said, rolling his eyes.

There was no way this woman was ever going to trust him, but if he was going to get the answers, he had to find some common ground.

"I tell you what, lady. Once we've figured out this mess, you can try and catch me. But until then, you need me. I fought this guy and lost, remember? You don't stand a chance without me, so get down off your Christmas tree."

"I don't trust you one bit," she retorted. "I don't want to work with you, but I guess I'm stuck with you. And my name is Agent Enhardt from now on."

"Fair enough, *lady*," Kellen said, not being able to resist getting in one last jibe.

He knew it must be getting late. The sun would be up soon and he wasn't ready for the public to see him patrolling during the day. If they were anything like Agent Enhardt, then he had a feeling that it wouldn't be a welcoming reception. In one aspect, she was right; to most people he would be classed as a freak. It was better that he remained in the shadows for now.

Victoria was trying to open the security barriers to get out. Kellen thought it was amusing watching her struggle, throwing out expletives every other word.

"Are you going to help me or not?" she snapped.

"Now you want my help." Kellen whizzed over there. He quested out for the electrical cables that operated the door. Raising his hand up, electricity shot from his fingers into the mechanism. The door slowly opened, cold air blasting him in the face.

He turned to Victoria. "There you go, free as a bird."

"Don't think that this changes anything. I'm going to be keeping a very close eye on you."

Kellen watched her leave down the giant corridor towards the front door of the museum. Part of him was beginning to like her. She may not trust him, but even heroes sometimes needed an ally. There was no way he could take on his enemies alone. Not yet anyway. He suddenly remembered something.

In a flash, he had caught up to her, putting his hand on her shoulder. She almost jumped out of her skin.

"I forgot to give you this," he said, passing her a small device in the shape of a V.

"What is it?" she asked, her brow creasing in to a frown.

"It's a com-link. If you press the button on the back, it'll send out a frequency that only I can pick up. Use it if you need to contact me."

Victoria said nothing. She just pocketed the device, walking away, leaving Kellen standing alone in the corridor. She would be a good ally, he thought, as he shot off in a blur. He had a feeling he was going to need all the help he could get.

Chapter Twelve

Kellen tiptoed into the back of his English Lit class, trying not to make a sound. The teacher had her back turned to the students. He was almost at his desk.

"Late again, Mr Amos?" Mrs Newman asked, turning to face him. "That's the third time this week."

"Sorry, Mrs Newman."

She placed her hands on her hips. "I'm afraid sorry just isn't going to cut it, young man. I'm going to have to write you a pink slip."

Great, Kellen thought, slumping down in to his seat. Another pink slip. He had grown quite a collection since his new career had started. A few more and he could create a papier-mâché sculpture out of them.

The late night patrols were beginning to take their toll. Four hours' sleep just wasn't enough, not with all the school work he was having to do on top of his 'other' work. He needed to find a way of juggling his everyday life with his hero persona. If he didn't find it soon, he was going to end up in a lot of trouble. He couldn't afford to be kicked out of school.

Mrs Newman handed him the slip.

"Don't let it happen again," she said. "Knuckle down and get your head out of the clouds."

"Yes, ma'am."

If only it were that simple, he thought.

***

Victoria sat behind her desk, chewing on the end of her pen. The computer screen was beginning to give her a headache. She had scrolled back and forth, up and down for the last three hours, going over the same evidence again and again. Nothing jumped out at her. It was clear that she was no closer to cracking the museum robbery case than she was to working out who was behind the mask. Zygonia City's newest vigilante had certainly left an impression on her.

She peered around the office. Her colleagues were too busy talking about the local football team or reading magazines to pay any attention. She opened her drawer.

There, sitting among paperclips and various other filing equipment, sat the signalling device. Would he come if she pressed it? She mused. She still wasn't sure if she could really trust him. For all she knew, he could still be responsible for the robbery. It wasn't like he was normal, going around dressed up like some kind of Halloween nut job. She wished she had questioned him more, tried to find out his real identity. But something in her gut told her he was the real deal and that he was going to play a big part in the events to come. She couldn't put her finger on it; there was just something about him.

"Hey, what are looking at, partner?"

Vinnie's voice broke her from her thoughts.

"Nothing, just going over the case files for the museum robbery."

"Any new leads to go on?"

Victoria shook her head.

"Well," Vinnie started, sitting down on the edge of her desk, "I may well have some news that'll please you."

Victoria looked him straight in the eye. She didn't want to get her hopes up; she'd gone over every inch of the evidence that they had. There was no way she could've missed something that her clown of a partner would have found.

"What?" she asked. "If this is one of your ploys to get me to go on a date with you, it isn't going to work. I don't have time for games."

"This isn't a game." Vinnie pulled out a piece of paper from his back pocket and placed it on her desk. Victoria scanned over it, her curiosity piqued. It had a list of dates and times on it.

"What does it all mean?" she asked.

"Well, we know the museum is owned by our local philanthropist, Mr Jonas. We also know that he would've been responsible for purchasing our missing staff for the museum's Egyptian display."

"Yeah, what's your point?"

"These are all the dates Mr Jonas flew out to, or conference called, his team in Egypt. He'd been working on this project for months. In secret. If all he had to do was purchase it, then why bother spending so much time and effort having a research team learn what they can from the staff? Why do it in secrecy?"

"That's all you got," she said, sitting back in her chair, dejected. "That means nothing. He probably had his research team checking to make sure the thing wasn't a fake."

Vinnie sat down closer to her on another chair. "Now wait a minute, I'm not finished yet. I thought the same as you at first, so I went back to our witness, the young boy that was the only one to survive. I visited him at the youth detention facility. And guess what?"

"For God's sake, what?"

"He remembers more about the unknown guy."

Victoria jumped up out of her seat and dragged her partner off into a quieter room. She spun on her heels. Furious.

"Why the hell didn't you tell me that you were going to interview him again?"

"You were too busy out there trying to chase after shadows. You've been obsessed with this masked vigilante since he came on the scene. One of us had to have our head in the game."

She paced around the room, still angry that her partner had gone behind her back. But she had to know what he'd found out.

"What did the guy say?" she asked, still pacing like a tiger trapped in a cage.

"Not much," Vinnie replied. "Same as last time. He kept going on about a guy with an eye-patch that had hired them all to do over the museum. He said that this guy was the one that killed them all. Said he had some kind of magical power. But..." Now it was his turn to look stern. "He said the guy was fast and his powers felt like static electric when it hit him. Sound familiar?"

"Now what're you talking about?"

"It has to be this Voltage guy. He's been taking out criminals left, right and centre, no doubt to get a leg up on the competition. Every single one of them that wasn't hospitalised mentioned speed and electricity when questioned. I said all along that he's dangerous. We need to talk—"

Victoria was already halfway out of the door. She'd heard enough.

"Hey, wait," Vinnie shouted after her. "Where're you going now?"

She didn't stop. "I'm going to try and attract some attention from our little vigilante."

Then she was gone.

***

Victoria climbed up the stairwell to the roof, sweat pouring down her back. The old apartment buildings were stifling, especially when the air conditioning wasn't working. But she knew there would be nobody else up there and she needed the privacy. She had a thief to catch.

She didn't want to believe the information Vinnie had given her, but the evidence was certainly pointing towards the contrary; she'd been wrong to trust someone in a mask. There was no way she was going to fall for it twice. This time, she would go through the proper channels; take him down to the station and get a statement. She put her hand to the gun in her shoulder holster. Locked and loaded. She was ready for anything.

When she reached the roof, she stepped outside. The bright sun blazed down on her, making her feel as though she'd stepped into an oven. Zygonia City was brewing for a storm.

Putting her thoughts aside, she took out the signalling device that Voltage had given her. She ran her hand over the V on its front. Smooth. Cold. She still wasn't sure if it would even work, let alone whether he would show up. Now is a better time to try it than any, she thought, pressing her finger down on the button.

Seconds passed. Then minutes. She pressed it two more times, but still nothing. She was about to leave when she heard a familiar whooshing sound. She spun around.

There he was, leaning up against a pole. Still masked.

"Sorry it took me a while, Agent" he said, taking a step towards her. "Some dude was trying to rob a grocery store. You know, you guys should really get down to the east side more. It's rough down there by the docks."

Victoria took a step back, whipping out her gun and pointing it at his head.

"Freeze!"

"Whoa, I thought we'd gone over this. I'm the good guy, remember?"

"Yeah, well that's what you led me to believe and if it's true, you won't mind coming down to the station to give me a proper statement. I never should've listened to you in the first place."

"Look, lady. That's not going to happen, so you may as well put your gun away and let me get back to saving lives." Voltage turned to leave.

"If you try to leave," Victoria shouted after him, "I'll be forced to shoot you and I really don't want to have to write *that* report up."

He turned back to her. "I'm on your damn side. Why can't you get that through your head?"

"So you say. There's still no sign of the other freak you mentioned. No records, no eyewitness accounts. Nothing, except an account from a kid that took such a beating I doubt he even knows what day it is. As far as I'm concerned, you're still the only person with superpowers around here and that makes you the number one suspect."

Voltage rolled his eyes. "Hooray for me," he said, sitting on the edge of the roof. "Do you really think that you're going to be able to take me in?"

"Yes."

Voltage laughed so hard he bent over double.

"What's so funny?" Victoria spat at him.

"For one, I'm a million times faster than you and could easily escape. And second, I'm not the guy you're looking for. He's out there and he's bad news. I told you that he kicked me into next week."

"But there's no sign of him anywhere. How do I know you're not lying?"

"Here we are," Voltage replied, rolling his eyes again. "Back to that trust thing."

The pair of them looked at each other, neither one moving. Trust had never been an easy thing for Victoria, but she knew she had to start sometime. The case was getting colder by the second; there were no other leads to go on. The sooner this is over the better, she thought. And if Voltage can help, then so be it.

She put her gun back in its holster. "What do we do now?" she asked.

Voltage stood up and faced her. He reached into the back of his suit, pulling out a flash drive. He knelt down, attached it to his wrist via a cable and then looked back up at her.

"Watch this," he said, as a screen projected from a tiny camera on his wrist and then onto the nearby wall. "Since I last saw you, I've been doing my own digging."

"Is that—"

"Yes," Voltage cut in before she could finish her sentence. "It's Jonas' manor house on the outskirts of town, and yes I was trespassing. Arrest me later."

Victoria gave him a clip around the back of the head.

"Ouch!"

"Carry on."

Voltage looked at her with scorn. Then looked back at the projection.

"Anyway," he continued, "I was doing some surveillance. I just had this feeling after I saw you that there was more to Jonas than meets the eye. He had to be involved somehow, but I didn't know how. It took me quite a while and a lot of late nights, but it paid off in the end. Does this guy fit your description?"

Victoria peered over his shoulder, staring hard at the image. It was dark. Grainy. But there was no mistaking the guy with the eye-patch and a huge scar down one side of his face. She stood up straight. It was all Victoria could do not to shudder.

"That's the guy I fought the other week. Now do you believe me?"

Victoria ignored the question. "I'm going to need that drive. The evidence you have is only circumstantial and the lab experts are going to have to go over the video footage to make sure that it's not fake. Don't think you're out of the woods yet."

She snatched the flash drive from his hand and marched over to the stairwell. This was it; all the evidence she needed to go straight to Jonas. She just didn't want this guy tagging along. He'd done a good job, she realised. But it was too risky. Time to let the pros do their job.

"You're welcome, lady," Voltage shouted after her. "I'll remember that the next time you need my help."

She didn't hear him. She was already halfway down the stairwell. Gone.

***

Victoria screeched the car to a halt outside the sparkling JonasTech building and jumped out in one fluid motion. She knew Jonas had influence, particularly in the police department, but she didn't care. Okay, she thought, the evidence is only circumstantial, but he had to be behind it. And there was no way she was going to let him squirm his way out of this one.

As she walked through the foyer to the main desk, heels clacking on the marble floor, butterflies began to flutter in the pit of her stomach. She knew she shouldn't be doing this alone, but if she took it back to the station the video would have to go through the proper channels. That meant there was a chance that Jonas, or his lackeys, would get wind of it and put a stop to any further investigation. It wouldn't be the first time. The department was rife with rumours of corruption, especially when it came to the higher echelons of Zygonian society. No, she realised, she was on her own.

"May I help you?" the receptionist asked as Victoria approached.

"I'm here to see Mr Jonas."

"Do you have an appointment, miss?"

"It's Agent Victoria Enhardt of the FBI," she replied, making sure there was just enough menace in her voice. She wasn't here to play games. "And I don't need an appointment."

She continued walking around the desk to the huge staircase in the middle of the foyer, ignoring the lifts to her right. It took the receptionist several seconds to register what was going on.

"S—Security!" the receptionist shouted. "Miss, I—I mean, Agent, you can't just go up there. Mr Jonas doesn't like being disturbed. You have to have an appointment!"

Victoria could feel eyes boring into her, but she didn't stop, just kept charging upwards. She knew exactly where his office would be. At the very top. Men like Jonas always think they're better than everyone else and, therefore, always put themselves on top of the heap. Well, she was about to bring this Tower of Babel crashing down around his ears.

As she reached the top of the stairs, two security guards were there to stop her. She flashed her badge and passed through them, heading straight for the two large double doors that she assumed would be the office she was looking for. She slammed them open.

"Ah, Agent Enhardt, I presume," Jonas said from behind his desk, his voice cool, calculating. "Allow me to introduce myself. I'm—"

"I know exactly who you are, Jonas," Victoria replied, cutting him off. "And I'm afraid you're going to have to come with me."

Jonas motioned to the two security guards. They left without hesitation, closing the door tight behind them.

"And why would that be, Agent?"

"I think you know why, Jonas."

He sat back in his armchair, eyes piercing straight through her. His arrogant smile was making her blood boil. Keep calm, Victoria, she thought. This is no time to lose it. Stay in control.

"Why don't you enlighten me," he purred.

"If that's the way you want to play it. We have an eyewitness account of the person that stole from your museum, and it just so happens that same person had been caught on camera going to and from your manor house. Little bit of a coincidence, don't you think?"

Jonas laughed. It was like nails scraping down a chalkboard. Victoria repressed a shudder crawling up her spine.

"Do you really think you'll be able to make that stick, Victoria? May I call you Victoria?"

"Agent Enhardt will do fine."

Jonas chuckled. "I'm one of the most powerful men in this city, Agent Enhardt. Now if you don't mind, I have things to do. This company doesn't run itself."

"I'm not afraid of you," Victoria spat at him. "Once I take you in and show my superiors the evidence, there's no way you'll be able to worm your way out of this one. It's over."

Jonas stood up, not once taking his eyes off her. He was still smiling. "You're a feisty one, aren't you? I could use a woman like you." He took a step towards her.

"Don't come any closer," Victoria said, her hand going straight for her gun. "I swear to God I'll shoot you."

Jonas began laughing at her again. Then, suddenly, his face screwed into a ball. He ripped open his shirt. Buttons flew off in all directions.

"Shoot me," he screamed, drooling like a madman. "Shoot me!"

"Get back, Jonas, or I swear I'll do it."

He grabbed a knife from his desk and flew at her. She reacted on instinct. The cocking action and the firing of the gun were carried out in one fluid motion. The bang almost deafened her. Now she'd done it, she thought. There was no way she was going to be able to explain this one to her chief.

But then she realised, Jonas was laughing instead of writhing around on the floor in his final death throes.

She couldn't believe what she was seeing. The bullet was just hovering centimetres from his heart, as if time had frozen. It was impossible. His mad laughter filled her ears. She couldn't move. Something was stopping her.

"H—H—How're you doing this to me?" she asked, the panic beginning to rise in her like a tidal wave.

"You didn't honestly think I would let you go, did you, Agent?"

She turned her eyes left and right, trying to find any means of escape. They widened in terror. A man with an eye-patch and a huge scar down one side of his face stepped out from the shadows. She was in way over her head.

"Victoria," Jonas said, "I'd like you to meet my associate. His name is Pulse."

Victoria could feel pressure on her head. It was making her dizzy. Sleepy. She was going to pass out any minute.

"You and I are going to have lots of fun."

Suddenly she felt the pressure release, freeing her body. She didn't waste any time.

Sprinting out of the door, she headed straight for the stairs. But stopped. Running down the stairs would be too easy for them to catch her. Steeling herself, she jumped into the lift.

Her heart was pounding as Pulse came rushing towards her. He disappeared as the doors closed, sending the elevator down. But it didn't ease her blood pressure. She hated them with a passion, having been stuck in one as a small child. Keep calm, she kept saying to herself. Keep calm.

Suddenly the elevator stopped. She could hear the blood rushing inside her ears. She had to get out to get help. But she was trapped. The air around her thickened. The walls closed in.

The lift shot back upwards like a rocket sending her sprawling to the floor. How was it possible? This was it, she thought. This is how it's all going to end, with me splattering all over the ceiling. She closed her eyes.

The last thing she heard before passing out was Jonas' maniacal laughter. Dammit, she thought. Why did Voltage have to be right?

Then nothing.

Chapter Thirteen

Kellen sat down behind his desk without making a sound. The rest of his classmates were sitting on their desks hanging out or goofing around. Just like young people his age should be, he thought with frustration. But he couldn't take his mind off Agent Enhardt. He should never have let her go off with the information on her own. Having only known her a short time, he was well aware of the amount of trouble she could get into. There was no way of telling what was going on with her, but even if there was, there was nothing he could do about it now. The professor had just entered the room and was about to begin his lesson. It would look a little strange if Kellen just upped and left.

"Okay, class," Professor Drake said, noting down an equation on the touch-board, "I've got a surprise for you today."

There was a murmur in the room as the anticipation of what was to come grew to exponential levels. A field trip, maybe? Some sort of competition? Kellen wasn't really that bothered. He had bigger fish to fry.

"We're going to be doing some practical work in pairs to solve the equation I've just noted down."

The excitement in the room turned to dismay. Every time the professor suggested doing work in pairs it meant pairing up with someone that you hadn't worked with before. It was part of the school's inclusion policy. Didn't they realise that young people only socialise through computers these days? No one wants to make small talk with someone they barely know, Kellen thought, as he moved his bag off the bench next to him.

He just sat at his station hoping that he would go unnoticed; the experiment would be finished quicker if he worked alone. That meant he could cut out early and get on patrol. Maybe he would be able to find Agent Enhardt. Wherever she may be.

***

"Is she awake?"

"She's coming around, sir."

The voices were faint, but Victoria could hear them through the haze of her unconsciousness. She could also hear water, which meant she was no doubt down by the docks. Damn it, she fumed. There was no way she was going to get out of this one. Nobody knew she was here. She didn't even know how long she'd been there. For all she knew, it could have been hours, or even days. Why hadn't she told Vinnie that she was coming to confront Jonas? She'd been so stupid to go alone, but it was too late for that now. She had to act. Fast.

Resisting the urge to open her eyes to see where she was, she tried to move her arms and legs, careful not to attract any attention. Nothing happened. She tried again. Nothing. She could only get about an inch of movement on each limb. That meant she was tied down to something.

Her heart began to pound harder in her chest. Panic was rising in her like a tropical storm. She took a deep breath, trying to calm her mind. Think, Victoria, think.

Then it came to her; the signalling device, it was in her pocket. All she had to do was try and weave her hand down, press it, then Voltage would come and whip her out of here.

She stretched her fingers out as far as she could. She could feel the device in her pocket. It was so close. She squirmed a little bit further, the tips of her fingers just centimetres away. She pushed harder. The cold metal felt good against her skin. Only a little further, she realised. After one final exertion, the palm of her hand was flat against the button. Now I've got you, she thought.

"What the hell are you doing?" a gruff voice called out.

Footsteps came rushing towards her and then someone grabbed hold of her arms. They were rough. They squeezed tight enough for her to let go of the device with a yelp.

"Get off me," she screamed, opening her eyes.

It took mere seconds for her to adjust to the sudden light. She soon wished she hadn't. It was like waking from one nightmare, only to be confronted by another.

Standing above her, snarling, was the man with the eye-patch and the scar. He put his hand in her pocket.

"Well, well. What do we have here, pretty lady?" he sneered, pulling out the device. The silver glinted in the fluorescent light. "You shouldn't have this."

"Who the hell are you?" Victoria asked. She'd already pressed the button. The longer she could keep him talking, the more chance it gave Voltage to come and save her.

"Name's Pulse," he replied, turning his back to her. "But you already knew that."

"What's that anyway? Some kind of lame gang name?"

He laughed. It made the hairs on the back of her neck stand on end. "I'll show you why they call me, Pulse." He turned to the guards standing by the door. There was a look in his single eye. Sick, twisted. It was like untempered fury. "Which one of you checked her for any tracking devices?" he asked the guards.

They both looked each other.

"Neither of you then, huh? Okay."

Victoria watched as Pulse turned his back to the guards. She had no idea what he was doing. The air pressure in the room began to increase, the static making her hair rise. She could see the concentration on his face. The guards were shaking. Her jaw dropped as a ball of energy began to form in his palms. Then he smiled.

Without warning, he spun back around and threw the energy balls straight at the guards' heads. They smashed against the wall with a loud crack. Then slumped to the floor.

Dead.

"Now," Pulse said turning back to her. "You going to tell me who you were trying to signal or am I going to have to rip it out of you?"

***

149

"Hey, stranger."

The voice almost made Kellen's heart jump out of his mouth.

"Is it okay if I work with you?" Linzi asked, taking a seat next to him.

"Um..." The words wouldn't come to him. He cleared his throat. "Sure."

The sweat was beginning to trickle down the back of his neck. He had no idea why he was feeling so nervous. He'd already spent some time with her at the science banquet. It wasn't like they'd never been together. Jesus, they'd kissed, he thought. Not that she knew it was him.

She smiled. The cogs in his brain were working overtime. He was pretty sure that if it had been a cartoon, smoke would be spewing out of his ears. She looked so beautiful with her hair down. Stop staring at her, you idiot, he fumed. Say something.

"So, um, did you have a good time at the banquet?"

"It was okay," she replied, filling up a jug with some kind of blue liquid. "I'm sorry you had to leave early. I never got to say goodbye."

"Yeah, I'm sorry about that too. I had to dash off for..."

Damn it, Kellen thought. There was no way that he could tell her the truth. For a start, it would make him look like an idiot, leaving an experiment running; and secondly, if he told her about the accident, she might work out that it was him that saved her at the jewellers. There was no way he could risk that happening.

"I, um, I was ill," he lied.

"Oh, dear. I'm sorry to hear that. Are you feeling better now?"

"Much better, thank you. In fact, I've never felt better. I'm as fit as a fiddle. Super-fit almost."

"Awesome."

The conversation dried up. Kellen felt like a complete idiot, babbling away about nothing. Here he was, the girl of his dreams sitting next to him, the perfect opportunity for him to get to know her better and to test the waters, but all he could do was mumble and talk rubbish. He needed to change the subject.

"H—How's your boyfriend? Jasper was it?"

"Casper. And don't ask."

Suddenly, his mind kicked in to high gear. Maybe they'd split up? That meant she would be single, which in turn meant that she was available for dating. As was he. It felt like the right time to push the subject. Kellen was almost seventy per cent certain that she'd been flirting with him. Maybe sixty.

"Oh no, are you two having problems?" he asked, trying not to sound as if he was overjoyed with the information.

"If it's all the same to you, I'd rather not talk about it."

"As long as you're—"

"Can we just get on with the experiment?" Linzi snapped.

Kellen did as he was told and got on with his work. A few moments of silence passed between them.

"I'm sorry," Linzi said. "I didn't mean to snap at you."

"That's okay. If you don't want to talk about it, we don't have to. I get it. You barely know me, so why would you want to talk to me about your personal life?"

"It's not that. It's just…" She let the words trail off as she tried to think of something to say. "Casper's finishing college early and going back to his hometown."

Kellen could barely keep his excitement under control. With the jock out of the way, it would leave the path clear for him to start a relationship with her. That's of course if she wanted to, he mused. It was about time things started to turn a corner for him. He'd been growing more and more frustrated with his situation and having his powers; he needed something else in his life. He was useless at being a hero. Perhaps he would be better at being a boyfriend? Let the feds take care of everything else.

"I'm sorry to hear that," he said, trying to hide the glee in his voice. "This mean you'll be breaking up?"

"I'm not sure yet. I think we're going to try the whole long-distance thing, but I'm sure you know how that usually ends."

They continued working for the next twenty minutes, chatting about school and work. When Linzi brought up the events from the jewellers, Kellen had to feign ignorance, pretending that he'd heard about it on the news. Lying had never been his strong point, but he was pretty certain that he'd pulled it off.

Linzi put her goggles on and grabbed a vial of red liquid.

"Are you ready?" she asked.

"Let's do it."

She poured the liquid into the jug containing the green gunge. Within seconds, it was frothing over the top like a volcano erupting. They both jumped back to avoid the mess.

"Well," she said, wiping some of the froth off of her jeans, "I don't think it was supposed to do that."

"I think not."

They both laughed. It was nice to finally take a break from all the hero stuff, Kellen thought. It was the first time in weeks that he hadn't felt so stressed. His newfound ease was making him feel confident.

"Hey," he started, shuffling his feet and staring at the floor. "Would you like to grab a milkshake sometime?"

"Yeah, sure."

"It won't be a date or anything. It would just be…" he said, trying to backtrack. He looked up. "Hang on. Did you just say you would go with me?"

Linzi was smiling at him. He'd never seen anything so cute in his life.

"Yes. I'd love to grab a milkshake. Maybe we could go after class?"

She reached out and stroked his arm. The electricity shot through him. He could feel his face going scarlet. She just laughed it off.

Suddenly, Kellen crumpled to the floor. A high-pitched noise was causing an unbearable pain in his head. The signalling device; the frequency must've been set too high. It felt as though his head was going to explode. Blood was beginning to drip out of his ears.

"Oh my God, Kellen, are you okay?" Linzi asked. Kellen could hear the panic in her voice.

He couldn't get up. Professor Drake came dashing over and put his hands on Kellen's shoulders to comfort him. But it made no difference. The pain was excruciating and was showing no signs of stopping. Not now, he thought, not now. Everything was going perfectly for him. He hated having these powers. All they'd done so far was get in the way. He'd had enough.

Closing his eyes, he took a deep breath, focusing his mind as hard as he could. He could pinpoint the source of the signal. He pushed his mind away from it. The noise was beginning to dim. It was working. Within a few seconds, he was in control again. The signal had gone dead.

He looked up. All the students had stopped what they were doing and were looking at him, some genuinely concerned, others with morbid curiosity. Linzi looked scared.

"You okay?" the professor asked, helping him off the floor. "Do you need to leave?"

"No," Kellen replied, somewhat shaken up. "No, I think I'm okay."

"Are you sure it's not an emergency? I can let you go if you need to."

He thought about it for a few moments. Deep down he knew he should check it out, but knowing Agent Enhardt it was probably just her way of getting him to come down to the station and reveal his identity; something that was never going to happen. She wasn't interested in working with him. All she wanted was his secret. Things were going too well for him in class. If he left, he would never have a life. There was no telling when he would get another chance with Linzi. She was the girl of his dreams.

"No, it's okay, Professor. It's nothing."

***

Victoria had lost count of the amount of times she'd passed out. It felt as though they'd been torturing her for hours. But she'd given them nothing. Voltage had never shown up. Never trust a man in a mask, she thought.

The guards and the man who called himself Pulse were talking in hushed tones. She had no idea what they were going to do to her now. She wasn't even sure she wanted to know.

Mr Jonas entered the room with an entourage. Pulse walked over to him. Victoria watched as they exchanged a few words. This is it, she thought. I'm useless to them, so they're bound to kill me. She was determined *not* to be easy game for them. Her father had always taught her to be a fighter and she was going to do him proud.

Jonas came over to the table she was strapped down to and stood over her, his ever-present, charming smile spread across his lips. It made her feel sick.

"And how are you doing, Agent?" Jonas asked.

"Never felt better."

He laughed before pulling the restraints tighter around her wrists. The leather bit deep into her flesh, causing rivulets of blood to run down her arm.

"My associate informs me that you were trying to signal for help."

It was more of a statement than a question. Victoria didn't answer. She was too busy trying to hold a scream in. There was no way she was going to give them the satisfaction of knowing they were causing her pain.

"Who was it?" Jonas asked, his voice dropping an octave. It dripped seduction.

Still she didn't answer.

Jonas laughed, letting go of the restraint. Victoria almost let out a sigh of relief.

"No matter. Soon there'll be no one left on this planet that can stop me."

"Slime ball," she spat. "When I get out of here I'm going to kick your sorry ass."

Jonas ignored her and walked back over to Pulse, his perfectly polished shoes echoing off the walls with each step. He took hold of the signalling device, looking over it. He pressed the button. Nothing happened. A look of scorn flashed over his face.

"Useless rubbish. It doesn't even work."

He started to walk out of the cavernous room with his entourage and then stopped, looking back at his lackey.

"I want her cleaned up and ready to go within the hour. We'll be moving onto the facility for the final preparations."

"Why are we taking her with us?" Pulse asked. "It could prove to be dangerous."

"You worry far too much, my one-eyed friend. Get it done."

With that, he was gone.

Pulse smashed his hand down hard on one of the metal tables, shouting expletives into the air. Victoria just lay still and let the other guards untie her.

She waited for them to slide her off the table before making her move.

Without skipping a beat, and using every last ounce of strength she had, she flung herself at the signalling device, slamming her hand down as hard as she could. It was worth another shot.

Suddenly she was hoisted into the air and thrown against one of the grime-encrusted walls. She landed on the floor in a heap, her head spinning.

Within seconds, Pulse was on top of her, yanking her up by the hair. When she looked into his eye, every ounce of fight she had left in her evaporated.

"Don't ever do that again," he said, dropping her to the floor and walking away. He turned to the guards. "If she's not ready by the time I get back, I'll kill you both."

As he left the room, Victoria looked at the other two dead guards by the door. It wasn't an idle threat.

***

"Kellen, I really think you should go and see a doctor," Linzi said, putting her arm around his shoulders. "This is the third time today that you've had one of these migraines."

"No, I'll be fine. Just give me a second."

They were halfway to the milkshake bar when the ringing had started again. Kellen was beginning to wonder whether it was in fact an emergency, but he couldn't just leave his date in the middle of the street; that would totally blow his chances with her. That is of course if he had any in the first place, he wondered, trying to ignore the sound.

"We can do this another day, if you still want to?"

He looked up at her, hope rising in him. Maybe he did have a chance after all? He'd left the agent sweating long enough. But he really was enjoying being in Linzi's company. Agent Enhardt could wait a little longer.

The sound stopped abruptly, as if it had been cut off. Panic rose in him like bile, forcing him to reconsider his plans. What if something bad had happened? It would all be his fault. No, he thought. Everything will work out okay. She was probably just checking in to share any more information she'd found on Jonas.

He looked at Linzi, trying his hardest to fake illness.

"Are you sure it's okay for us to do this another time?" he asked. "I'm really not feeling too well."

"Of course it is. You get back to the dorm. I can make my own way home from here."

"I really am sorry about all this."

"Don't worry. It'll make the next time all the more enjoyable."

She smiled and kissed him on the cheek, turning his face bright pink. He looked like some kind of neon sign.

Happiness coursed through his veins. He just stood there, a vacant expression on his face like a lovesick puppy.

Linzi giggled. "Get going before you collapse."

Her voice broke him out of his thoughts. He gave her one last smile and then walked off in the opposite direction, looking back over his shoulder, grinning from ear to ear. The evening hadn't turned out that bad after all.

Then he remembered the signal.

Getting himself together, he looked around for the nearest dark alley so that he could change. He spotted one and made his way over to it as fast as possible without looking conspicuous. His eyes darted about to make sure he wasn't being watched. It was empty.

In a blur of motion, sparks flew all around as Kellen went from being a normal teenage boy to the masked vigilante known as Voltage. In a way, a part of him enjoyed being in the costume. He certainly couldn't say that he lived a boring life, despite his recent frustrations and the responsibilities his powers had put on him.

The last thing he could remember about the signal was sensing it in the direction of the docks. Without hesitation, he sent his mind out and absorbed some of the electricity from the nearby power lines. He didn't need much before he could feel it building in his centre. The static made the hairs on his arms stand on end. The suit was doing its job, making it easier to conduct the electricity.

A grin spread across his lips. Then he shot off at the speed of light.

It took him seconds to reach his destination. The signal had been coming from one particular warehouse.

"Okay," he called out, as he barged into the open room. "This had better be…"

The last word caught in his throat. The warehouse was completely empty, devoid of any sign of Agent Enhardt.

His eyes darted about.

Then he spotted it. A giant bloodstain in the middle of the room.

"Oh crap."

Chapter Fourteen

Kellen felt like a failure. He slumped down against the slime-encrusted warehouse wall not knowing what to do next. Victoria was out there somewhere, she had to be. He wouldn't let his mind contemplate the other possibility. His senses quested for her; any remote sign. But nothing. She had trusted him and he had let her down all because he had taken too long to decide. Now he had no idea where to start looking for her. His incredible speed meant nothing. Time was running out.

In the distance there was a heavy rumbling sound. Was it thunder? Kellen wondered, climbing to his feet. That was all he needed; bad weather to remove any sign of the agent that he could track. Not that he knew how to track, he realised. For the first time since the accident, he realised that he had been relying on his powers to catch the criminals on the street. Now they were letting him down, his lack of ability as a true crime fighter was showing.

The noise was constant and grew louder as he approached the behemoth of a window flanking the iron walkway that ringed the inner wall of the building. He could see nothing, not even the normal fishing boats coming out from the harbour. That was weird, he thought. The little fishing boats were always out in the bay.

Suddenly the noise grew to a crescendo. Brilliant white light flooded through the window, blinding him and causing him to cover his eyes from the glare. He couldn't see a thing.

"Hands up, this is the police," a voice boomed across the harbour. "We have the place surrounded. You are strongly advised to come quietly."

Now he could hear sirens coming from all directions. Even with his powers, he wasn't sure if he would make it through a blockade. He was trapped.

***

Vinnie sat the megaphone between his feet on the floor of the helicopter. Excitement flooded his body, causing the hairs on the back of his neck to stand up.

"We've got him now, Joe," he said, patting his co-pilot on the shoulder.

Any minute now, the net would tighten around Zygonia's masked vigilante; then Vinnie would get the answers he was looking for. By force if necessary.

Victoria had been missing since she'd left the station yesterday. Since then nothing. She hadn't checked in at all. If it hadn't have been for one of his snitches suggesting he search at the docks, he'd have no idea where to look. He was positive the freak hiding inside the warehouse would provide more answers.

From his vantage point in the helicopter he could see the ring of squad cars forming around the building. Soon the

SWAT teams would be in position and then it would be all systems go. This was the first time he had ever lead a full-scale operation. He could feel the excitement rising in the air. He lifted up the megaphone.

"I repeat, this is the police. We have the building surrounded. Please remain where you are until officers enter the building to escort you to the station. Any attempt at escape will be met by force."

Now everything was in place. A triumphant glint in his eye sparkled with the moonlight. The radio microphone crackled with static as he spoke into it.

"This is Big Daddy from Eagle Eye, are all units in position?" He paused waiting for a reply.

"That's affirmative. All units are ready for go."

This is it. His moment to finally shine. He'd made a promise that he would look out for his partner and she needed him now. He would make her proud by putting all that goofing around behind him.

"Don't worry, Vicky, I'm coming for you," he whispered to himself, before placing the microphone against his lips. "All units close in."

***

Kellen had to think fast. If he tried to run, then there was a chance that a sniper may take a shot and hit the jackpot; that was something he couldn't afford to risk. That meant fighting his way out. He certainly had enough juice left in him to make a stand and fight, but that would mean hurting innocent people that were just doing their job. Could he really afford to cross that line? It was a line, if crossed, that he could never come back from. There had to be another way.

Outside, he could hear the helicopter hovering overhead, its occupant blaring through a megaphone informing him of his impending doom. All he had tried to do since the accident was help people. Now those same people thought of him as a criminal – a murderer to be hunted and persecuted. Professor Drake had been wrong; this wasn't a gift, it was a curse.

His gloved fist slammed hard against the damp wall, sending bright blue flashes in to the air. Tears fell from his masked eyes as the frustration overwhelmed him. There was no way he was cut out for this hero stuff; it had been stupid to even try and pull it off. What did a science geek know about being a hero, even if he did have superpowers? Muggers were one thing; they didn't stand a chance against him. But whoever had taken Agent Enhardt was something else. Now she was in serious danger because of his playing at cops and robbers.

Deep down Kellen knew it was all connected to the mysterious scarred man from the alleyway. There had to be a way of finding her, he thought, wiping at his eyes. A grim determination had set in his jaw. He may not be a hero, but Victoria was alive, he could sense it. His fists clenched. He wasn't going to let her down again. But first he had to get away from the warehouse.

With his mind clear, a thought struck him. Helicopters would have a radio system, which meant whoever was in the helicopter was probably the one leading the assault on the building. A simple radio was no problem to plug into.

Kellen sent his senses racing through the millions of invisible signals hanging out in the air, frantically trying to pinpoint the right one. Come on, he thought. Time was running out. Any second the assault teams would be bursting into the cavernous warehouse. Suddenly he picked up the signal.

That is affirmative. All units are ready for go.

He had it. That had to be the right one. Within a second, he had managed to jam the outgoing signal from the helicopter. Now all he had to do was try and explain what he was doing here.

All units close in.

"Sorry, buddy, but that's not happening today," Kellen said with a confidence he didn't feel. "Now, I don't know who you are, but you have to listen to me."

"Like hell I do. Repeat, all units move in."

"Look, they can't hear you. It's just you and me."

"Oh, I see. One of your freak tricks. I made a promise and I plan to keep it. You may have jammed the radio, but there are other ways to communicate."

Damn, Kellen remembered the megaphone. If the officer used that, there would be no way for Kellen to stop them. Then he would have to fight.

"Please, listen to me. I don't want anybody to get hurt. I know you think that I've kidnapped one of your officers, but I haven't. I'm trying to save her."

A few seconds passed.

"Yeah, right, and I'm the Easter Bunny. That's my partner you have in there, sicko!"

"Vinnie?" Kellen asked, hoping that familiarity might make a difference.

"How do you know my name?"

"Victoria told me all about you. I know you think I took her, but you're wrong. We've been working together trying to crack the museum case. I'm not the only person in this city with powers."

"What? That's just rubbish. No more stalling. We're coming in."

"Wait, you have to believe me. If you ever want to save her then you're going to need me to do it."

There was another pause before Kellen heard the slick voice in his head again.

"How do I know I can trust you? This could all be some elaborate ploy to escape."

"Victoria trusted me, now you have to."

Big Daddy, this is unit one, are we ready for go?

"So, Big Daddy," Kellen said, a hint of sarcasm in his voice. "Are we going to work together? The mike is open for you."

Again there was a moment's silence. Kellen held his breath.

This is Big Daddy, false alarm, guys .I guess we all get to go home and watch Melrose Place *now.*

Kellen closed off the radio signal again. "Thank you."

"Don't thank me, just get out there and find her. But I swear, if you're lying to me then I will do everything in my power to hunt you down and destroy you. Is that understood?"

"Yes, sir. I won't let you down."

He wouldn't let them down either. Not again, he thought, as he sped off into the moonlit night, long shadows crawling over his dark determined face.

***

Dan sat slurping his milkshake on the bottom step of the dorm, bathing in the warmth from the sunshine. He was hoping to catch Kellen. His friend seemed to have no spare time at the moment and when he did, he was distracted and distant. It had been since the accident in the lab; something must have happened that night that was playing on his mind, Dan thought, taking another long gulp. He was supposed to be his best friend and it was his responsibility to make sure he was okay.

Spotting Kellen marching across the quad broke his train of thought. There was a look about his friend that didn't sit right. His back was rigid, his fist clenched and his jaw was tight, as if he was chewing a wasp. Dan picked himself up off the front step and began to stroll forwards, his ever-present smile beaming like the sun. As Kellen approached, he put his hand up in greeting.

"Hey, man, how's—"

"Sorry, Dan, not now. I haven't got time," Kellen replied, marching straight past.

Dan was stunned. It was as if his friend had just slapped him in the face. There was definitely something amiss, but Dan was dammed if he knew what it was. He quickly moved to catch up.

"Dude, what's wrong? You're acting all weird."

"I've just got things to do, that's all."

"Maybe I can help? You look like you haven't had a wink of sleep all night."

Kellen spun on his heels, a livid fury in his eyes.

"Look, Dan, if you can't accept that I have things to do that *don't* involve you, then that's your problem. Unlike you, I have responsibilities."

Dan just stood there in disbelief. Where had all the anger come from? He had no idea what Kellen was talking about.

Before Dan could even find out what the hell was going on, Kellen had started to march off in the direction of the science labs.

Getting more and more frustrated, Dan caught up for a second time and yanked his friend around by the shoulder. It was his turn to do the shouting.

"What do you mean you have responsibilities? I know you want to do well in class and impress Linzi, but I'm your friend, Kellen, and I'm worried the pressure is getting to you."

"Pressure? You don't know anything about pressure."

"Kellen, this isn't you talking. I want to help you, man, but I can't if you won't explain," Dan said, a look of real concern filling his eyes.

"There's nothing wrong. Please, just leave me alone."

With that Kellen was gone, leaving Dan standing alone with the last dregs of his milkshake.

"Fine! You do whatever it is that you think is so important, but don't expect me to still be here when you've finished. We're done, dude."

There was no reply to his last outburst, so with his head bowed low, he walked off in the direction of his own dormitory.

Chapter Fifteen

Kellen stormed down the office corridor, his jaw clenched tight. Small bolts of electricity flashed behind his eyes like a storm was raging inside. Keeping his head down, so as not to arouse the suspicions of the people to-ing and fro-ing along the corridor, he headed for Professor Drake's room. He could feel the raw power behind the walls, beckoning him to reach out and unleash his fury. How dare Dan think he could monopolise his time?

As he rounded the corner, he pushed the thoughts to the back of his mind. Dan would just have to get on with his little temper tantrum, he thought, approaching Professor Drake's door. He had more important things to do now; responsibilities that couldn't just be forgotten on a whim. His recent actions proved that.

Without knocking, Kellen burst through the door. "Professor, I need your help."

"Why not just come right on in," Drake replied. "Knocking never hurt anyone."

Kellen noticed the reproach, but chose to ignore it. "I need to break in to a police office."

"Now hang on a minute, sit—"

"There isn't time!"

Kellen slammed his fist down hard on the polished oak surface of Professor Drake's desk. Instantly, every electrical appliance and plug socket in the room blew out in a cacophony of miniature explosions.

Several moments passed before the professor rose from his seat, quietly surveying the damage to his office. Outside in the corridor, a chorus of panicked workers had begun to pick up, wondering where the sudden commotion had come from. He went out into the corridor to calm them, claiming that it was just an electrical surge from a small experiment he was working on. Kellen just stood there, horrified that he had lost control. What if he had hurt someone? It was yet another failure he could add to his ever-growing list.

Drake closed the office door and sat back down behind his desk, his face expressionless as he stared straight at Kellen. No words were spoken. Seconds ticked by in silence.

"I'm sorry, Professor."

"I just don't know what's happening to you. You've been skipping classes, dropping grades. I think explanations are in order, don't you?"

"Look, I really am sorry that I lost control, but I don't have time to sit and have a chat with you about my problems. The FBI agent I've been working with has gone missing. I think she's been kidnapped."

"Now again, slow down. What agent?"

Despite losing his patience, Kellen started from the beginning. He explained how he had been working with Victoria on cracking the museum case and how he had received a distress call from her but had taken too long to run to her rescue. The story just tumbled from him as if the words were a torrent of water cascading down a cliff face. By the time he had finished, the full weight of his responsibilities dragged him down to his knees, his face buried in his hands.

"I've failed everyone, Professor. I'm not cut out to be a hero. I'm just a nerdy physics student. Now because of me, someone is in danger. I have to help them, but I can't do it without you."

Small sobs shook his frame as Professor Drake came around and picked Kellen up off the floor. He looked him dead in the eye.

"Everything is going to be okay. As a scientist, I don't believe in fate, or destiny, but you've been given a gift. It may have been an accident, but in my eyes, there is no one more suited to be a hero than you. Everybody struggles with life's pressures. You're still human after all."

"But I failed. I chose to have a life and ignored someone in need. That sound like a hero to you?"

Professor Drake took Kellen by the shoulders, a look of concern flashing across his eyes.

"Kellen, listen to me. I know you didn't ask for these responsibilities, but you have them now and nobody can change that. We can't always pick and choose how we want our lives to turn out and you're a prime example of that. You have to finish what you've started, son. Then you can have your life back."

"But what if she dies? It'll be my fault, Professor."

"We can't afford to think like that. You must put everything aside and focus on the problem at hand. Only you have the power to save her."

Professor Drake stood back and waited for Kellen to pull himself together. He sat back down behind his desk. Kellen took a deep breath.

"I know that Agent Enhardt was keeping this one close to her chest. The last thing I heard from her was that she was chasing up on a strong lead that I gave her. Then she vanished. But I think I know how to find her."

"Okay. So, how can I help you? I believe you said something about a police office?"

Kellen leant across the desk, sparks dancing at the corners of his eyes. Everything rested on him. If his plan didn't work then Victoria would be killed along with thousands of others including those he loved most. No matter how he felt about his newfound responsibilities, he wouldn't let that happen. It was a daring plan, one that would be difficult to pull off. But it was the only chance he had.

"We're going to break into the police station."

***

Night had long fallen over the city. A gentle quiet had blanketed over the tall apartment buildings and office blocks that made up this end of town, with their dim lights twinkling in the darkness as people went about their lives oblivious to the growing storm that was waiting around the corner. But for Kellen, it was a different matter.

He stood on top of one of the tallest buildings, looking out over Zygonia City. Something deep down told him that this museum robbery was going to lead to something big. Something bigger than him. He shook his head.

"What's wrong?" Professor Drake asked. "You've been staring out over the city for the last ten minutes."

"I was just thinking about things. About how things have changed so much so quickly."

Drake stepped forward. "Remember what we talked about earlier? Now isn't the time to dwell on what might be. You have a job to do and I know you'll see it through." He rubbed his hands together. "I think we should start making a move."

"Not yet," Kellen said, looking back in the direction of the police station. "I'm waiting for a signal."

"What signal? Kellen, you haven't even told me the pla—"

Before Professor Drake could even finish his sentence, Kellen had hoisted him over his shoulder and was super-speeding towards the other end of the building. They stopped just short of the edge.

"Kellen, what the hell is going on?" Drake shouted. "I demand you put me down this instant and explain to me how we're going to get into that police building when you're a wanted man."

"Easy," Kellen replied, smiling for the first time since Agent Enhardt had gone missing. "We're going to jump."

He absorbed as much power as he could from the surrounding buildings as the professor protested. Lights started dimming. He could feel the raw power surging through his body as it began to vibrate his molecules.

"Have you ever even tried this before?" Professor Drake screamed.

"Umm, nope. Hold on tight."

Kellen unleashed a surge of power that propelled them across the rooftop. Just before they hit the edge, he vaulted over the stonework, sending the two of them flying through the air. The pedestrians and cars below were oblivious to the two men flying overhead, the engines and car horns blocking out Professor Drake's panicked shouts, his eyes shut tight.

The two of them landed on the police station roof with a dull thud. Neither of them were injured.

"Jesus, that was some mean feat," Vinnie cooed, stepping out from the shadows. "Our files on you really need to be updated."

Kellen stood up and brushed himself off.

"Thanks, but we haven't got time for that. Let's get—"

"Whoa, kid, I'm putting my neck on the line for you," he said, grabbing Kellen's arm. "So you better be on the level. Who's the old guy?"

"I'm Professor Drake, head of the physics department at the Zygonia School of Excellence, and we'll have a little less of the old, if you don't mind. There's a good chap."

Vinnie looked at Kellen.

"It's all right. Professor Drake's the only person I know capable of hacking into Agent Enhardt's files."

"But—"

"But nothing!" Kellen could feel his fists starting to clench. He took another deep breath to calm himself. "Look, I'm sure you want to find your partner as much as I do and for that to happen we need the professor."

Vinnie took one last look at Drake and then back at Kellen.

"Okay," he sighed. "Follow me. We don't have much time."

The three of them entered the building via the roof, following Vinnie's lead.

"Won't your colleagues wonder why Zygonia's most wanted man is walking around the halls?" Professor Drake asked.

"You'd think so, right?" Vinnie replied, as they stepped into the brightly lit hallway of the top floor. "But as you can see, since our masked vigilante here's been around, the cops have been pretty lax in showing up for work; especially on the nightshifts. You're putting us out of business, kid."

There was a deathly silence along the short hallway as they made their way towards the stairs. It was as if they were the only ones in the building. Vinnie's voice seemed to just bounce off of the walls.

"Victoria's office is down on the next floor. Now, you two won't have much time to get your thing done. We can't take the chance of anybody coming along and spotting you in that get up." He stopped and looked Kellen up-and-down, shaking his head in disapproval. "Couldn't you have picked a better costume?"

"I'm sorry, I'll just pop back to my hidden cave and change. Can we just focus and stop worrying about my costume?"

"Oh yeah, where was I?"

"You were explaining how it would be foolish for Voltage here to get caught," Professor Drake replied with an air of annoyance.

"Okay, so I'll wait out in the corridor just in case anyone comes along. That way I can most probably keep them off your back."

"Probably?" Kellen asked. He looked at the professor, who also had a worried expression furrowing his brow.

"Okay, almost definitely. Is that any better?"

Kellen sighed. This is going to be a long night, he realised, as they rounded a corner onto the stairs.

The corridor below them was just as bright and just as deserted as the previous one. The soles of Kellen's boots squeaked on the polished tiles with every step as the trio made their way to Victoria's office. Vinnie pulled out a set of keys and unlocked the door.

"Knock yourselves out, guys. Just do it fast."

Kellen and Professor Drake wasted no time. They closed the door, shutting out Vinnie and got to work. After ten minutes they still hadn't managed to hack the system.

"Professor, this is taking far too long. Can't you go any faster?"

"Haven't you learned anything from me, Kellen? Patience is a virtue that will yield results." He looked over at his troubled student. "Besides, not all of us have been blessed with super-speed."

Kellen could hear the reproach in his mentor's voice. He felt so ashamed of himself for snapping. He just couldn't help it.

"I'm sorry. I just feel so useless at the moment, Professor. Is there anything I can do to help?"

"Maybe you could zip around the room and see if you can find anything that might give us a clue as to the agent's password."

Within seconds, Kellen had blitzed the entire office. Debris from his search lay littered all over the room. He slumped down in the desk chair. Defeated.

"Nothing. Absolutely nothing!"

Professor Drake swivelled around in his chair.

"It's just as well I know my way around a firewall then, isn't it?"

"What?" Kellen asked, confused.

"I'm in."

He whizzed over to the computer table, looking frantically over the professor's shoulder.

"Have you found anything?"

"Well, it appears that Agent Enhardt has been keeping very detailed files on you. I can delete those for now, but you're going to have to be careful in the future."

Kellen could feel his cheeks turning red under his mask. "What about the museum robbery? Is there anything on there that could tell us where she might be?"

"I can't find anything related to the robbery. No e-mails, no files, no clues. Nothing. There's plenty of information on all the other cases that she's been working on. But it's as if she'd never been working on this one."

Great, Kellen thought. Another dead end. Zygonia was one of the biggest cities on the eastern seaboard; without a lead to follow, it would be like trying to find a needle in a haystack.

"There has to be something, anything."

"I'll keep looking."

Kellen took another whizz around the office. Just as he was about to give up, the door to the office suddenly opened. Vinnie's worried face peered around the corner.

"Guys, someone's coming."

"Well, stall them," Kellen hissed. "We need more time!"

"Just hurry it up already."

And with that he shut the door. Kellen raced back over to the professor.

"Anything?" he asked, his voice almost frantic.

He could feel the sweat pouring down the back of his neck underneath the leather suit. It was causing the static to crackle every time he moved. He could hear Vinnie's voice. He was joking around with his colleagues in an attempt to distract them. If I get caught, it's curtains, he realised. That couldn't happen.

"I think I found something."

The professor's voice snapped Kellen back into reality. "What is it?" he asked.

"It was hidden inside another encrypted file, deep in the hard drive." He turned to face Kellen. "It's a dossier on JonasTech. It appears that the agent has had suspicions on the company for quite some time. When you gave her the flash-drive, it seems you gave her the final ammunition she needed to arrest him. There's evidence of embezzlement, illegal arms trading, corruption with the highest authorities. You name it, it's on here. I think she's suggesting that the museum robbery is one of a long line of staged heists. Mr Jonas owns the museum. It wouldn't be hard for him to pull it off and keep his public image intact."

Kellen could feel his heart rate rising. He'd been right about the heist all along. Why Agent Enhardt hadn't shared her suspicions with him was a mystery. But it didn't matter now, he realised. He would get Victoria back and put an end to all of the upheaval in his life. Then he could be with Linzi.

"Thanks, Professor. I take it you'll be able to make your own way back to the school?"

"But, Kellen, wait—"

Before Professor Drake could finish his answer, there was a loud sonic boom and Kellen was gone. The office door swung on its hinges.

"Good evening, officers," Drake said, smiling at the bewildered men in the corridor. "Would you mind giving me a lift back to the school?"

***

Like a man possessed, Kellen shot off in the direction of the JonasTech building, zigzagging in and out of the busy traffic in the entertainment district. His mind was now fully focused on the task ahead. There was no way he could let this go on any longer. It had to end.

Within minutes, his destination loomed large in the distance, quiet and foreboding. He could feel a churning in the pit of his stomach. He knew the best approach would be to go in silent. Undetectable. But his temper had got the better of him – something that had been happening a lot lately. Was it a side effect of his powers, he wondered. Whatever it was, he would deal with it later. There were more important things to deal with first.

The large double doors leading to the foyer flew open as Kellen entered the building. Two security guards jolted upright, startled by the sudden interruption of their card game.

"Sorry to do this, guys. I'll try to be gentle."

Before they could react, Kellen shot out tiny sparks to knock them out. He sped over to them and caught them before they hit the floor. No point in going over the top, he thought. These guys probably don't even know that they're working for a scumbag.

He took a quick look at the map behind the desk. Jonas' penthouse was on the top floor. No doubt there would be other guards lurking around, so he would have to be quick.

Sending out his senses, he absorbed the electricity from the nearby PC terminal. It wouldn't hurt to have some backup power, just in case, he mused. He pushed out further, connecting to the police radios. No one had alerted the police of his break in, so he was still undetected in the building. But it wouldn't be long. An APB had been put out for him after he had shot off from the police station. Damn, he fumed. I should've been more careful, but at least they don't know I'm here.

Suddenly, he felt woozy. There was another energy signature in the building that he'd felt before. He put his hands out on the desk to steady himself. What the hell is that, he wondered. He shook his head to clear the sensation. No doubt it was something to do with one of the many experiments that they carried out in the labs. Pushing it to the back of his mind, he shot off in the direction of the penthouse.

Kellen burst through the doors.

"Jonas, where are you?" he shouted.

"He's not here."

Kellen spun around in the direction of the voice.

Pulse stood behind the desk, his single sinister eye fixed on Kellen.

"You took your time," Pulse said, his voice steady. Menacing. "I've been expecting you."

He shot out his hand. Kellen knew what was coming, but he couldn't dodge it quickly enough. His legs flew out from under him as his body smashed against the far wall. He landed in a heap on the floor with an audible groan.

Without skipping a beat, he flew towards Pulse, aiming a quick punch at his head. But his assailant blocked it with ease, throwing out another psychic push. Kellen again found himself on the floor. Man, this guy's strong, he thought. I've got to be quicker.

He quickly shot a ball of electricity at Pulse, but again he just deflected it with his hand. Kellen was running out of power.

Pulse just laughed at him, strutting over towards his prone form. His shadow fell over Kellen.

"I've been at this a lot longer than you, boy."

He put a swift kick into Kellen's ribs.

He gasped for air. With every breath, his ribs screamed in agony, no doubt broken.

"You won't get away with this," he said to Pulse's back through gritted teeth. "I'll stop you."

"Hmm, yes, I'm sure you will," Pulse replied, sitting back down behind the desk. "Look, kid, I hate Jonas just as much as you, but I made a promise to an old friend and I plan on seeing it through. It would be better for everyone if you just—"

The sentence was cut short, as he was flung over the back of his chair by an electricity ball. Kellen rose to his feet, jaw clenched, eyes burning with fury.

He sped over to Pulse.

"Where's Victoria?" he asked, straddling his enemy and punching him in the face with every word. "Where is she? Tell me!"

"Ha-ha. Nice try, pup. But I don't need my hands to use my powers."

Again Kellen was thrown across the room, this time landing through a table. Tiny splinters pierced his suit through to his body like little bee stings. This time, before he could do anything, he could feel a choking around his neck as he was hoisted in to the air.

His lungs screamed for oxygen as the corners of his vision began to blur.

"That was a good effort," Pulse remarked. "Not many people catch me off guard. I can guarantee it won't happen again."

He slung Kellen through the large TV screen, shattering it into a thousand tiny pieces.

Kellen could feel the energy evaporating from him. He had failed; again. Pulse stood above him.

"Looks like round two goes to me. Better luck next time, pup. Not that there'll be a next time."

A searing pain shot through Kellen's head. He writhed around on the floor in agony, screaming at the top of his lungs. Every muscle twitched and tightened as if he had some form of extreme cramp. His connection to the electricity grid was dimming. What the hell's going on, he wondered. What's he doing to me?

"I was told to kill you," Pulse said, as Kellen's vision began to blacken. "But I have a better idea."

One final pain shot through Kellen's body.

"Night night, pup."

Then darkness.

Chapter Sixteen

Kellen awoke prone on the office floor. He lay there for a few moments just staring at the white ceiling, waiting for his blurred vision to clear. His head pounded. It was the second time he had taken a beating from the mysterious silver-haired man, he realised. Pulse was it? It was a fitting name considering he had flung Kellen around like a Frisbee with his sonic blasts. He winced at the memory.

Several minutes passed before he finally dragged himself off the floor, grimacing with the effort as his muscles spasmed and his bones groaned. Pulse had really put him through the ringer this time. But at least now he knew what he was up against. A grin spread over his masked face and with it came a new sense of determination; he knew how to find them.

Kellen hobbled over to the window and looked out over the rooftops as they glinted in the orange hue of the early morning sun. During the fight he had managed to attach a tracking device to Pulse's jacket. Now all he had to do was send out his senses, reach for the tracking signal and find them wherever they were. The plan couldn't fail; he would find them, speed in and rescue Victoria so that she could alert her special task force. Together they would take down Jonas before he could wreak havoc with the staff. And then Kellen could get his life back, just the way it was. Well, not exactly the way it was, he thought. This time he would get the girl.

He closed his eyes, questing for the tracking signal.

His brow began to furrow. He couldn't sense it, so he pushed harder. Nothing. The pounding in his head intensified. No matter how hard he pushed, there was nothing there. Was the tracking beacon broken, he wondered. Maybe it had been switched off?

A sudden thought struck him. He pushed out his mind, searching for the smallest spark of electricity. Panic surged through his body. But no power.

Kellen stopped questing. There was only one thing left for him to do. He took a deep breath and ran.

Then fell flat on his face.

His legs just didn't seem to want to move fast enough. Somehow, Pulse had managed to switch off his powers, making it impossible for him to access the source of his speed.

Kellen picked himself up off the floor. How the hell did he do this, he thought, his mind racing through the possibilities. How am I going to find them now? There's no way I can beat them without my powers.

Then he stopped. Maybe he didn't have to stop them. He never asked for the powers in the first place, nor the responsibilities that came with them. Jonas was a police problem, not his. Now he was free to get on with his life and put it all behind him. Except for one problem.

He wasn't that guy.

Having abilities had changed him somehow. They had made him a better person – more confident and sure of himself. They had given him another purpose in life. He wanted to help people that couldn't help themselves. It was true. He *had* lost his way. But not because of his powers. It was because he hadn't known how to handle them. Now they're gone, he thought, I want them back. He wasn't just the science geek any more. He was more than that. He was a hero.

But to do it, he would need help. He had to get back to school. Fast.

***

It took Kellen over an hour to get back to school through the traffic. The cab driver had done his best to weave in and out of the other cars, but it had been painfully slow. He hadn't realised just how much he relied on his super-speed to get places these days. It was just one more thing he had taken for granted. And it wasn't just his powers he'd lost. He'd had to ditch his uniform in favour of some maintenance clothes from one of JonasTech's labs. He couldn't afford to be seen wearing that. The last thing he needed was to be arrested.

Thankfully, the school seemed pretty quiet. The large clock in the centre of the court said it was only seven o'clock in the morning. Jesus, he thought, I've been out all night again. Jonas and his lackeys could be anywhere by now. That meant it would be even harder to find Victoria. That's providing she was still alive.

He pushed the thought to the back of his mind, not wanting to dwell on the thought that he may have been responsible for the death of a good cop out of his own selfish behaviour. It made him angry. All this time he had been trying to ignore the fact that things were different and not wanting his powers. Now, at a time he really needed them, they were gone. He didn't even know where to start looking in order for him to get them back. Or even if he *could* get them back. His brain refused to even think about what would happen if he didn't. It wasn't an option. Somehow, no matter what it took, he would find a way.

"Whoa, sorry, I… Oh, hi, Kellen. Are you okay? I was totally away on another planet."

Great, he thought. If there was one person he hadn't wanted to bump into it was Linzi and yet here she was, looking more beautiful than ever in her jogging gear.

"H—Hi. I'm fine thanks, how're you?"

Linzi gave a coy smile, noticing Kellen's nervous stammer.

"I'm great," she replied, brushing her dark curls away from her face. "Missed you in class though. Professor Drake said you were still unwell."

Kellen could feel his cheeks getting brighter by the minute. "Yeah, I—I—" Stop stammering you idiot, he thought. "I haven't been well at all."

"Nothing serious, I hope?"

He could see her eyes sparkling in the early morning sun. She looked perfect. It was a shame he didn't have the time to hang around and talk.

"Look, I've really got to get going." Kellen brushed past her. She grabbed his arm before he could get any further.

"Have I done something to upset you?" she asked. "You seem really off and you've been avoiding me since you dashed off the other day."

"It's not that. I've just been really busy with… stuff."

"Like what?"

He could see she was getting annoyed now, standing there with her eyes glaring at him, arms crossed. He rolled his eyes.

"I don't have time for this!" he exclaimed.

"Well make time," Linzi replied. A crestfallen look fell over her face. "I thought we were friends?"

"Look, I've got so much on my plate right now."

"Fine. Have it your way." Linzi spun on her heels and started marching in the opposite direction.

"Linzi, please wait."

She turned back to face him. "For your information, Casper and I broke up yesterday." She looked him up and down. "But I guess that doesn't matter any more."

Then she was gone. Kellen watched her disappear around the corner, his heart feeling like it had been stomped on. Heavy footsteps and panting broke him out of the moment.

He spun around to face the source of his disturbance.

"Dude," Dan said, bent over double and gasping for air. "I spotted you out of the window and ran down here as fast as I could. God, I'm cutting down on cheeseburgers. One second."

Kellen rolled his eyes. "Not now. I'm busy."

"Yeah, about that. We need to talk."

"There's nothing left to say."

Dan cocked an eyebrow. "Except you left out the part about being a superhero."

***

Victoria's head pounded as her eyes fluttered open, slowly adjusting to the bright halogen lights overhead. She had no idea how long she'd been out for. Hours? Days? Weeks? There was just no way of knowing. They must've knocked me out again, she realised. She should never have trusted the vigilante to come and save her. She had learnt early on in her career to only trust herself.

As she went to move her arms, handcuffs bit into the tender flesh around her wrists. She was chained to a metal chair that was beginning to make her legs go numb.

Fantastic, she thought. Even if I could pick the lock on these cuffs, I wouldn't be able to run very far if I wanted to. Out of instinct, she began looking around for an exit. There wasn't any. She was alone in what appeared to be some kind of underground cell. Everything around her seemed to smell… clinical; the kind of smell that you tend to get in hospitals, or science labs. But then who would build a science lab or hospital underground? None of it was making any sense. What the hell have you got yourself into this time, Vicky, she mused.

Footsteps from down the corridor snapped her out of her thoughts. She kept her eyes fixed forward, jaw clenched, as if she wasn't fazed by being kidnapped at all. Deep down, her heart was racing.

"She's awake."

The man motioned to two other military-looking types. One of them stepped forward and opened the cell, while the other began unlocking Victoria from her bonds. Her wrists felt as though they'd been rubbed raw, but she couldn't take her eyes off of the man that had spoken. Pulse.

"Hey, buddy," she said as she was yanked to her feet. "Take it easy there. I'd hate for you to have to lose some teeth."

The guard scoffed at her before shoving her out of the cell and along the corridor. Her eyes bore in to the back of Pulse's head.

"So, what're you supposed to be, a pirate?"

"You should know by now that I'm your worst nightmare if you try to escape."

Victoria struggled to hide the shiver that ran up her spine when her captor spoke. His voice was cold and emotionless; a man used to killing, she realised. But how was he connected to Jonas? No doubt she would find out soon enough.

She remained silent for the rest of their short walk through the complex. But once they reached their destination, her jaw dropped. She was inside a giant cavern, which was housing some of the most advanced equipment she had ever seen in her life. It was as if she had been teleported to another planet; one far more advanced than her own. Scientists scurried to and fro along the walkways like albino wasps, their white jackets flapping out behind them as they dashed about to complete their tasks. Bright lights illuminated every nook and cranny of the cave. At the centre was a machine she couldn't even begin to understand. It was like some kind of giant MRI scanner. And it was exactly where she was being led to.

As they reached the bottom of the walkway, she noticed that the staff from the museum was being attached to the machine. She watched as scientists fixed it into position. The figure stepped forward from behind a screen.

"Ah, Miss Enhardt, so glad you could join us."

"Jonas, why have you brought me here?"

"Well, my dear, you seemed very interested in my business. So I had Pulse here bring you to our wonderful new facility."

She watched as Pulse bristled at Jonas' words. There was certainly no love lost between the two.

"Cut the crap, Jonas. What's all this got to do with that staff?"

"Aren't we a feisty one?"

Jonas walked over to the contraption holding the staff. His hand caressed the smooth surface as if it was the most precious object in the world.

"This staff contains the ultimate power." His eyes gleamed as he spoke. "Whoever can harness its abilities could rule the world."

Victoria's eyes widened. If Jonas has found a way to harness that power, then she wasn't the only one in danger. He was the type of crazy that wouldn't stop at ruling the world. He'd destroy it.

"Oh, and you think that machine will do that for you?" she asked, trying to stall the proceedings.

"I have every faith. The world's best scientific minds have been working on this for months. In fact, here's the man of the hour now."

Victoria turned her head and saw who Jonas was talking about. Dr Rollingson was half shuffling, half being dragged into the space around the contraption. He was bedraggled and looked like he hadn't slept in days.

"Doctor Rollingson, you can't help this monster," Victoria implored.

The doctor turned his sad eyes towards her. "I'm sorry, miss, but I don't know who you are or how you're caught up in this. Believe me when I say that I had no choice. He threatened the life of my daughter."

"There's always a choice."

"I would love for you two to carry on with this little conversation, but time is running short." Jonas motioned to the doctor. "If you wouldn't mind."

Pulse pulled Victoria to one side as the rest of the lab technicians began strapping Jonas into the contraption.

"Now, Agent," Jonas began. "What this machine does is act as a conduit for the power locked in the staff. When I'm strapped into it, the good doctor over there will switch it on and I will become a god. That has such a nice ring to it, doesn't it?"

"You won't get away with this."

"Oh? And who's going to stop me? Your pet superhero, perhaps?" A sinister laugh erupted from him, echoing around the room. "I'm afraid he's been dealt with. Isn't that right, Pulse?"

"Yes, Mr Jonas."

Victoria's fists clenched behind her back. If Voltage was dead, then she had to think fast. Preparations for whatever was about to happen were still going ahead. Time was running out. She looked at the man next to her. "I can see you don't get along with him," she said. "There's still time to stop this. Do you really want him to have more power over you than he already has?"

Pulse turned his single eye towards her. She could see, for the first time, this was a man torn between doing the right thing and his honour.

"Not all of us have the luxury of choices," he said, his voice now softer. "I made a promise once and if I'm anything, it's a man of my word."

Victoria suddenly felt the restraints around her wrists go loose. She looked at Pulse dumbfounded. How did he do that, she wondered. More importantly, why?

"Besides, there's still hope."

She didn't understand what he meant. There was no one left that could stop the madness. Preparations had finished. Time had run out.

"Doctor, switch on the machine."

Victoria watched as an electrical current ran through the staff. A loud whirring noise filled the cavern, deafening her. All around her, static began to crackle. The computer running the machine suddenly exploded. The staff above was beginning to glow.

Jonas lay strapped to the machine, half-laughing half-howling, as the light beam flashed up and down his body.

Then he burst into flames.

Victoria covered her ears to block out the screams. This had to stop.

The flaming ball grew outwards, scorching the solid grey floor. Flames lashed out with fury in all directions. The searing heat caused her to cover her face with her arms before a sudden eruption blasted everyone off their feet.

Then it went quiet. Nothing moved.

After a few moments, Pulse managed to rise to his feet, still dazed from the blast.

Victoria opened her eyes. In the middle of the room, Jonas was untouched, his naked body facing away from them.

"Mr Jonas, are you all right?"

"Where am I?" Jonas asked in a booming voice that reverberated off of the walls.

"You're at the facility, Mr Jonas."

"Who is this Jonas creature you refer to?"

Pulse stepped forward. "He's you, sir."

"I am no mere mortal, worm. I am Raman the Destroyer." He spun to face Pulse, his eyes blood red, a crown of flames leaping from the top of his now-bald skull. The two men locked gazes. "And you will all kneel before me."

For the first time in his life, Pulse lowered his head and trembled. Victoria silently prayed to God to save them. Jonas had succeeded.

The end of the world had come.

Chapter Seventeen

Kellen and Dan sat opposite each other in silence. The entire dorm room was still, neither one of them knowing what to say to the other. Kellen had no idea how his friend had found out about his new abilities; it's not like he had been broadcasting them over the airwaves for all to see. As far as he knew, the police and Professor Drake were the only ones that knew of his extracurricular activities and not even the police department knew his true identity. He felt stupid. How long had Dan known? Why hadn't he said anything sooner? Part of him was screaming to know more, to bring it all out in the open and demand that Dan tell him where the information had come from. But part of him realised that his friend must be feeling the same way.

"Look Dan, I—"

"Look, dude…"

The two of them looked at each other, both feeling awkward.

"You first," Dan offered.

"I—I don't know where to start. Everything's been so crazy that most of the time I haven't known whether I've being coming or going." Kellen looked at his friend, sincerity in his eyes. "I wanted to tell you all along, I just didn't know how."

"Is it permanent? Are you in any danger?"

"I don't know. As far as I can tell, I don't think so. Professor Drake has been running all kinds of tests on me, but even he can't really tell the effect it's having on my body. It's been a very steep learning curve."

"Dude, why didn't you tell me earlier? I could've helped. I don't know in what capacity, but I'm sure I could've been useful in some way. Everyone always sees me as the goofball. No one ever trusts me with anything serious. It sucks."

Kellen jumped up, hurt by his friend's words. "How can you say that? You're my best friend and I would trust you with my life. But this is different. It's not like I could've walked up to you one day and said, *Hey Dan, how're you? Oh and by the way, that accident last night gave me superpowers.* You would've thought I was nuts!"

This time it was Dan's turn to seem shocked. "Bro, this is me you're talking to. I would've seen it as the most awesome thing to ever happen in the world, period. How often is it a guy can turn around and say that his best friend is a superhero?"

"Not often, I guess," Kellen replied, turning to face him. How had he ever doubted the man standing next to him? Shame washed over him, so much so that he turned to look back out of the window. Rainclouds were gathering on the horizon. "Thanks, Dan."

He felt a gentle hand on his shoulder turn him around.

"That's what friends are for. Besides, every good hero needs a sidekick. I'm thinking we could call me Bistro Boy. My superpower; eating. A lot."

The two of them laughed at the joke, shattering the tension that had built up between them. Everything had been forgotten. For the first time in what seemed like an age, Kellen felt as though a giant weight had been lifted from his shoulders. Keeping the secret all to himself had been harder than dealing with the changes in his life. Professor Drake knowing helped, but it wasn't enough. Now his best friend was there to share his worries and his doubts. Now he could concentrate on being a hero.

"Dan," Kellen started. "How did you find out about me?"

"It wasn't all that hard. After you ditched me, I—"

"I never ditched you," Kellen cut in, stung by the accusation.

"Dude, you so did, but it's cool, I get it. Places to go, a world to save and all that." Dan paused for a moment. "Where was I?"

"I'd ditched you. Apparently."

"Oh yeah. So, after you *ditched* me, I came back up here to think things over. The news was on TV and that's when it hit me."

"How?"

"They were showcasing Zygonia's new man of mystery. You got caught on the security cameras at the museum. They're putting the heist on you, calling you a masked menace and asking citizens to be vigilant. I think the cops're getting desperate."

"I'm the least of their worries."

Kellen was disturbed by the news. If the police were getting the citizenry involved, then it would make moving around the city difficult. But there was one more question he had to ask, one that was even more important.

"How did you know it was me? It could've been anyone in that costume."

Dan raised an eyebrow. "Dude, I've known you for, like, ever. I could spot you a mile away. Put that with your erratic behaviour lately and it's really not that hard. You're like a brother to me, which is why I could see it, but I don't think anyone else could tell it was you."

Kellen sat in silence for a few moments, not knowing what to do next. Maybe he would have to rethink his uniform in the future. Either that or learn to black out all the security cameras.

"So," Dan said, breaking the silence and sitting back on the bed. He made himself comfortable before continuing. "How did this happen?"

Kellen went right back to the beginning of his tale, starting with his strange visions the night of the accident. His friend hung on every word. It felt good to get it off his chest. He felt free. It took him over an hour to explain the whole thing.

"This is so cool," Dan said, almost falling off of the bed in his excitement. "So, what kind of things can you do?"

Then it hit Kellen like a freight train. Victoria was still out there somewhere and here he was, laughing and joking, wasting more time. He had let his life come between him and his duties again. He didn't even know whether she was still alive.

He jumped up. "Dan, I'm really sorry, I've got to go."

"Whoa, settle down, where's the fire?"

Kellen's mind was racing. No matter what it took, he had to get his powers back, find Victoria and stop Jonas. He didn't have time to explain.

"You know the agent I mentioned, the one I've been working with?"

Dan nodded.

"Well she's in trouble and I have to save her before it's too late. Jesus, she could be dead for all I know."

Dan jumped up and grabbed his friend by the shoulders.

"Dude, slow down, you're not making any sense. How is the agent in trouble? Maybe I can help."

Kellen took a deep breath. Maybe it was time he trusted someone other than the professor.

"Do you remember that night at the science banquet?" he asked. "That creepy guy from JonasTech sat with us."

"The CEO? Yeah, I remember him. Didn't like him much."

"He stole the staff from the museum. The heist was all a big elaborate hoax and Victoria found out. She signalled for me when she confronted him, but I... I ignored her."

Dan stood and thought for a moment. Suddenly his face lit up.

"Okay, why don't you just use your powers to get her back?"

"That's the problem," Kellen replied. "Jonas has some kind of superhuman henchman. He's powerful. I've fought him twice now and both times I've lost. I don't know how it happened, but the last time he managed to switch off my powers." His eyes turned to the floor. "They're gone. And I have no idea how to get them back."

Dan looked more determined than ever. His jaw locked together and his eyes were stern.

"I'm going to help you, man. I don't know how, bearing in mind I have very little physics knowledge. But together, we'll get your powers back."

"But how? I have no idea how it happened in the first place except that it was something to do with the accident."

"I have an idea, but first," Dan said, smiling. He took his friend by the shoulders. "We're going to need a professor."

***

"Out of the question," Professor Drake said, jumping out of his seat. "Absolutely not. I will not allow it."

"But, Professor," Kellen replied. "It's the only chance I have of getting my powers back. Surely it's worth a try?"

The professor walked around his desk and stood in front of the two boys. Dan looked a little sheepish, but Kellen stood his ground. If he didn't act now it would be too late and the last thing he wanted was the consequences of that laying on his shoulders.

"It's too dangerous to recreate the accident, Kellen. To be honest, we have no idea which part of the accident gave you your powers, so to recreate it would be impossible anyway."

"But with your help, I know we can do it. You're one of the world's leading physicists."

Professor Drake took Kellen firmly by the shoulders. "No. It can't be done."

"But, Professor, pl—"

"No, I'm sorry, boys, but my word is final. I will not put either of you at risk."

Just when Kellen thought he couldn't get any lower, he hit rock bottom. Even Dan standing beside him looked downtrodden. But there was something else bubbling beneath the surface. Anger. How could the professor dismiss the idea? He'd been with Kellen since the beginning, helped him control his abilities and had even encouraged him to become a hero. Now he was asking him to walk away when the world needed him most. Kellen just couldn't understand it.

Professor Drake sat back down behind his desk. "Now, I know it's hard to walk away from this right now, but this has got way out of hand. I know you did your best, Kellen, but things are far too dangerous from what you've told me. These aren't just street thugs any more. This is a man who has the ability to hurt you, if not kill you. I do not want to be a part of that."

The anger in Kellen began to dissipate. He could see that it was taking every ounce of the professor's strength to get through this conversation. For the first time in a long while, he could see how much the man had become a father-figure to him.

He looked around at Dan, who had remained silent throughout. The two of them exchanged acknowledging glances.

"I think that the two of you should get down to the police station and explain everything to them," Professor Drake said, breaking the silence. "Come clean about being Voltage. It's a risk, but it's one I'm sure you're willing to take."

Kellen nodded. "Okay, Professor."

"Good."

Drake ushered the boys over to the door. He took Kellen by the shoulder before he left.

"It's for the best, you do know that, don't you?"

"I guess so."

"Agent Enhardt is better off having professionals trying to find her than us. You did your best and I'm proud of you. Now you just need to have faith. Whatever Jonas' ultimate goal is, the authorities will deal with it. Can you let it go?"

"I'll try."

"Good lad."

Kellen and Dan left the office and made their way outside. The sun had dipped behind the clouds and small drops of rain were beginning to splash on the dry, grey concrete pavement. Neither one of them spoke for several minutes.

"Well," Dan said, catching up to his friend. "I guess that's it. What're you going to do now?"

"We go to the police like the professor said. Let them deal with it all."

Dan didn't answer, but Kellen felt a tug at his arm. He spun around to see what was wrong. His eyes followed Dan's arm, pointing out towards the horizon.

In the distance was a grey smudge growing out steadily into a cloud. Kellen couldn't work out what it was at first and then he realised. Smoke.

More and more smoke clouds were springing up across the horizon of the city, blocking out the normal sight of skyscrapers and offices. His heart was racing. What the hell is happening out there, he wondered. Gas pipe explosion? If only I had my powers, then I could zip over and help out. But he was useless. There was nothing he could do now except find a TV and see if it was on the news.

He turned to Dan, about to tell him that they needed to get back to the dorm room. Suddenly the earth shook beneath them and a ball of fire erupted in the distance.

Dan's jaw dropped.

Kellen's fists clenched.

They looked at each other, both nodding in agreement.

The city was under attack and there was only one person in the world capable of saving it. They had to get to the lab to get Kellen's powers back, with or without the professor.

Chapter Eighteen

"Fall back, fall back," Vinnie screamed at the decimated ranks of officers behind him.

The army that was attacking Zygonia City had come from nowhere. One minute he'd been flirting with a female officer by the water cooler, the next it had come over the radio that the city was under attack. Now he was watching officers die right in front of him. Where the hell was Voltage?

A cop went down next to him, blood frothing from his mouth. He leant down to help him. "It's okay," he said, trying to sooth the dying man. "You're gonna be all right."

"I—I've been h—hit. T—Tell my g—girlfriend that I—I love her."

"I will."

The man's eyes glazed over as death took him. Vinnie gently closed his eyelids before wiping tears out of his own eyes. What the hell was happening? How had it come to this?

He stood up, surveying the chaos. Officers fell, people ran, buildings toppled. It was like a scene from a war movie. Even the army reserves were struggling to stay together. Bit by bit, they were pushing the enemy back. But it wasn't enough.

Then he saw it in the distance.

A mechanised platform was making its way down Main Street, flanked by an army the likes of which he had never seen.

Throngs of skeletal warriors armed to the teeth were hacking and slashing at anything that came in their path. Nothing was stopping them. Guns weren't working. It was going to take a miracle to win this one, he realised.

Getting down on to one knee for the first time in years, Vinnie prayed for salvation. Somewhere out there was Victoria. He prayed that wherever she was, she wasn't seeing the devastation.

***

Victoria stood in chains at the vanguard of the mechanised platform, hovering down the main boulevard of Zygonia City. She watched as an army of un-dead soldiers tore through the streets. Every now and then, cannons at the rear of the platform would burst in to life, peppering the nearby buildings with large fiery explosions, each one tugging at her heartstrings. She loved this city more than anything in the world and she could do nothing except watch it die.

Terrified citizens rushed to and fro in an attempt to get out of the way. If the soldiers didn't get them, the heavy cannon fire did, engulfing them in flames. The acrid stench of smoke clawed at the back of her throat, choking and clogging her lungs each time they passed another decimated store front. Where the hell is Voltage, she wondered.

"Your thoughts betray you, woman," Raman said, his voice soft, seductive. "Who is this Voltage that fills your mind?"

"He's someone that can kick your ass."

"I doubt that very much. I have conquered whole civilisations, decimated entire armies with a mere fraction of my power. One tiny mortal will not halt my plan."

Victoria stood there, a small chuckle escaping from her lips. It grew until it became full-blown hysteria.

"You dare mock me, woman?"

"You're no different from any of the other scumbags I've taken down in my time. You all have delusions of grandeur, thinking that you're some unstoppable force. Well, in my experience, there's always a bigger fish out there."

Raman turned towards her, his cloak billowing in the ash-streaked wind. He bent his head until it was level with hers. His thin lips pulled back into a sneer.

"You doubt my power. Then maybe I shall show you a taste of what I am capable of."

He marched to the front of the platform, arms outstretched. His left-hand knuckles turned white as he gripped his golden staff tighter. In the distance, two tanks were beginning to form up underneath an archway that was supposed to mirror the Arc de Triomphe in Paris. Long blue streaks of lightning crackled in the air. Windows shattered, sending shards of glittering glass clattering to the floor. The platform stopped. Raman began chanting words in a language Victoria didn't understand. She held her breath.

Without warning, a loud boom erupted from the ground beneath the archway. Huge blocks of marble crashed down onto the two tanks, trapping the men inside. Other soldiers were crushed, killing them instantly. Victoria looked away.

"No, no, my pretty. You will learn to revel in my power." He motioned for Pulse to make her watch.

As he came behind Victoria, Pulse bent forward closer to her ear. "I'm sorry," he whispered. "It'll be better for you if you just submit to his wishes. It'd be better for all of us."

"No," Victoria screamed, as he forced her head forward. "You won't win. Someone'll stop you."

Then her heart almost skipped a beat. In the distance, behind the rubble that was once one of Zygonia's greatest monuments, was the prep school campus. Thousands of kids would be in there.

"Again your thoughts betray you," Raman said. "It's a nice building. Maybe I'll make that my new palace."

"No, you can't," Victoria cried. "It's full of kids that've done nothing to you."

"Then I will have more slaves, won't I?"

Raman whipped around, stopping inches from her face. She could smell his putrid breath. She couldn't help but stare into his black soulless eyes.

"You will learn to fear me."

His booming laughter echoed in her ears as she was forced to watch the platform move closer towards the school.

***

"Are you sure this is going to work?" Dan asked, his brow furrowing. "It all sounds a little risky to me?"

"I know," Kellen replied, as they both rushed down the corridor towards the lab. "The only way I know how to get my powers back is to recreate the accident that caused them in the first place."

Dan grabbed his friend by the shoulder. He looked him straight in the eye. "But you barely survived last time. What if you die? I really don't think I'd look good in a slave outfit."

They both laughed, more out of nervousness than anything else. Kellen knew that Dan was right. He was taking a huge risk. But it was the only way.

He looked out of the window to his left. More black smoke was billowing into the sky, making the city skyline look like a war zone. Having the powers had turned out to be a curse rather than a blessing. Now he realised that he needed them more than ever. Without them, everything he knew and loved was doomed. He was the only one who could stop the chaos. He had to get them back; no matter what.

He looked back to his friend, trying his best to look calm and confident.

"Look, Dan. You've been the best friend anybody could ask for and I can't say the same for myself."

"Don't do it. I know that look."

"Am I that obvious?"

"Yes, you are. So don't you go trying any of your tr—"

Before Dan could finish, Kellen shoved him backwards and darted off in the direction of the lab. As he reached it, he slammed the door shut.

"Hey," Dan shouted, hammering his fists on the newly fixed glass. "You've got to let me in. I can't let you do this on your own. You know I'm always up for any wacky scheme, but this is far too dangerous. There's no telling what it could do to you this time."

It was no good. Kellen was ignoring him. He hammered harder on the door. "I broke this glass once before, I can do it again. I may be fat, but I'm like the Blob when I get going. Now open up."

Still nothing. He watched his friend rushing backwards and forwards past the window like a madman.

"Goddamn it, Kellen, open this door."

Kellen finally stopped. Dan could see that he had poured the super conducting serum all over himself.

"Please, buddy, don't do it. There has to be another way. Let the authorities deal with it. As much as I hate to admit it, we're only kids. This is too big for us."

Kellen just stood there.

"Can you even hear me through this?"

Before Kellen could answer, a loud explosion in the quad rocked the entire building, making the plaster fall from the ceiling. Both of the boys looked at each other through the glass.

"Was that you?" Dan asked.

Kellen shook his head.

Dan quickly rushed back towards the security station at the front of the building. As he rounded one of the corners, he bumped into something soft. He stumbled backwards, tripping over his own feet.

He looked up, a relieved smile lighting up his face.

"Thank God. Am I glad to see you, Professor. You've got to help me stop Kellen. He's going to recreate the accident to get his powers back."

"Against my orders?" Professor Drake asked.

Dan picked himself up off the floor. He grabbed the professor by the sleeve and began to drag him down the corridor.

"That's not important. The important thing is we stop him from doing—"

"It's no good. If Kellen doesn't get his powers back, we're all doomed."

"Say what now?" Dan asked, looking confused. The whole thing was starting to give him a headache.

"We're under attack. Without Kellen, none of us are going to get out of this alive. I was wrong to deny him my help. I see that now."

"Look, I know the city's under attack, but—"

"I'm not talking about the city," Drake said, pulling Dan along to the main entrance and shoving him outside. "I'm talking about the school."

Dan looked around at the half-demolished buildings and the hordes of un-dead attacking his schoolmates. He made the sign of the cross. "Holy crap, we're under attack."

Then he fainted.

***

Kellen ducked down behind the windowsill, peaking through a gap in the blinds. He watched as the student body of The Zygonia School of Excellence was herded like cattle into makeshift holding areas on the quad. The armoured soldiers were beginning to search the buildings. It wouldn't be long before they checked the labs. He had to do something. And fast.

Just as he was about to move, he spotted the platform moving back towards the main entrance, flanked by the horrific un-dead. It wasn't hard to work out who was in charge. In the middle, sitting on a huge golden throne, was a bald man with a fiery crown, dressed like an ancient Egyptian, holding onto a staff. It was the same staff that had been stolen from the museum three weeks ago. And standing next to him, being held in place by Pulse, was Victoria. Thank God she was still alive, he thought, muttering a prayer under his breath.

He stared hard at the platform as it made its way out of the school grounds. He could stop this madness, he knew it. All he needed was his powers back.

Crawling along the floor, he made his way over to the nano-electromechanical ion drive.

He took a deep breath. This was it, he realized, reaching out for the main switch. He couldn't take his eyes off the window and the men marching around outside. They could spot him at any minute.

His fingers brushed against the lever.

Male voices caught his attention outside the door. He couldn't hear what they were saying.

His hand gripped the lever.

They were beginning to smash on the glass.

He brought his hand down.

***

Dan groaned as his eyes flickered open.

"Where the hell am I? What happened?"

"You fainted is what happened, fat boy."

He looked around at the source of the voice. It was Zach Lietzke.

"What're you staring at me for, fat boy? You think I'm a doughnut?"

"Hey, leave him alone," a female voice shouted. "You think this is funny? We're all in trouble here, so just shut the hell up."

"Ooh, what're you going to do, little girl?" Zach sniggered.

Dan looked around in the direction of the second source. It was Linzi. She was making her way through the throngs of shaking bodies. Students, frightened out of their wits.

She marched straight up to Zach and punched him square in the face.

"That's what I'm going to do."

She walked over to Dan. As she reached him, she put out her hand to help him up.

"Someone's needed to do that for a long time," she said, looking at Zach holding his bloody nose on the floor. "You okay, Dan?"

Dan looked down at the prone Zach on the floor. He turned back to Linzi. "I've been better. What's going on here?"

"I don't know. Some strange army led by a guy dressed as an Egyptian pharaoh came marching in here and took the school. We're all being corralled into these little holding pens. But I have no idea why."

Dan looked around. The mechanized throne was getting ready to move off. He could see the soldiers marching around, checking each and every building for stragglers. The city must've been ablaze. The bright blue sky had taken on a greying-orange hue from all the smoke and fire. Loud gunshots could be heard in the distance. He looked back at Linzi.

"Have you seen Professor Drake? He was with me when I, um, fainted."

Linzi pointed towards the platform. "He's over there with that woman being held prisoner on the platform."

Great, now they'd lost the professor. He hoped Kellen would hurry up and do whatever it was he was planning on doing. Things were beginning to go from bad to worse.

Suddenly the platform repulsors burst into life, sending warm air rushing out into the surrounding people. Students began to whimper, afraid of what was going to happen next. As it hovered past their cage, it stopped. The Egyptian-looking guy gazed straight down at Linzi.

He stepped forward.

"I know this woman," Raman said, pointing down at her. "Bring her to me. I would have her witness my conquest of this city."

The macabre, skeletal hands of the un-dead grabbed her by the arms.

"Hey, get off me. What do you think you're doing?"

Dan jumped into action.

"Yo, dead dude," he shouted at one of them. "Take that." He threw out a meaty fist, smashing the skull clear off one of them. The soldier staggered back as Dan waved his hand about in agony.

"Jesus, I think I broke my hand. They make it look so easy in the comics."

Linzi kicked the other one in the shin and ran over to Dan, grabbing him by the shoulder.

They struggled through the crowd, trying to get away. Students had begun to fight back. Fists, helmets and bones flew through the air. The pair pushed and shoved their way past, forcing a gap to open up in the crowd. There were too many of them.

"This is useless," Linzi cried over her shoulder. "We're never going to get out of this."

Dan clutched at his hand. "It's okay," he replied. "Kellen will get this all sorted. You just wait and see."

"What's Kellen got to do with all of this? Where is he anyway?"

"Um, well he, um… He's working on something."

"Like what?"

"Look out!"

Suddenly the pair of them were hoisted into the air by unseen hands. Dan was tossed to one side as Pulse lowered Linzi onto the platform. All the time Raman was bellowing laughter: Psychotic, sadistic laughter. The platform began to move off.

More soldiers were rushing towards Dan. This was it, he realised. He was going to die a virgin. He'd always pictured himself dying old, probably from a heart attack. Instead he was going to be beaten to death by some goons that belonged to a guy that looks as if he should be at a comic book convention. He was no hero. Jesus, he thought, he wasn't even great at being a sidekick. It wasn't even worth trying to fight back.

He closed his eyes and waited for the onslaught.

A loud explosion made him reopen them. The soldiers had stopped in their tracks, unaware of what was happening. But Dan knew.

He smiled at them.

"Now you're going to get it."

Chapter Nineteen

Kellen's eyes flickered open. The acrid smoke from the super conducting serum burnt the back of his throat. He remembered the experiment hurting a lot less the first time it had gone off. He felt sick. Weak. He knew he had to move, but his body wouldn't do as it was told. Soldiers were scrambling around in the debris, trying to find their feet just as he was. If they got up before he did then it was all over. Come on, he thought. You've got to move.

He managed to push himself up onto his knees. The whole world felt as though it'd been tipped on its side.

"Freeze," a soldier barked at him. "Move and you're dead."

"Trust me, pal. I'm not going anywhere."

The soldier turned to one of his comrades. "Bind him up and take him out to the others." He turned to leave but then stopped and turned back. "Oh, and tell the captain that it was just some stupid kid that caused the explosion."

"On ya feet, scum."

The soldier pulled Kellen up by the collar of his shirt. His head pounded.

"Hey, watch it," he said as the soldier nudged him in the back with the butt of his gun, almost tripping him up.

"Oh, the tough guy, are ya? Well, you ain't gonna be so tough when Mr Jonas, or should I say Lord Raman, gets a hold of ya. I'll tell ya that for free."

Kellen stopped in his tracks and looked around at the soldier. "Mr Jonas?"

"Yeah, numb nut, Mr Jonas; the wealthiest man in Zygonia City. Who else do ya think could pull off something like this?"

"That's enough, Soldier. Just get him to the pens."

"Yes, sir!"

Everything was falling into place. Jonas had been planning this all along, Kellen realised, as he stepped out into the fading sunlight. No doubt he'd had his scientists working on a way of unlocking the power of the staff for months. Through his wealth, he'd bought it for the museum just so he could send in his lackeys and steal it. The whole heist had been a ruse to throw people off his true purpose. Why had he not seen it all before? Kellen wondered. For someone that was supposed to be a genius, he felt pretty stupid. Not only that, recreating the accident hadn't given him his powers back. He had no idea where his friends were. All he felt now was alone and numb.

The soldier shoved him into a makeshift cage. "You better get comfy. You're gonna be here for a while." The soldier walked away laughing, leaving Kellen to glare at him. He looked around. Frightened faces stared back as if he was an alien. They must have been kids from the year below; most of them looked like they weren't even old enough to be at high school.

He knelt down in front of one young girl. "Everything'll be okay," he said, trying to sound as reassuring as he could. He certainly didn't feel it.

Looking around outside of the cage, he could see the chaos left behind by Raman's army. In the distance, he could still hear gunshots and explosions.

Slouching down against the bars of the cage, he couldn't bear to think about what was going on out there. He closed his eyes. Why hadn't his idea worked?

For the first time in as long as he could remember, he wept.

***

"Do you see the power I hold at my fingertips?" Raman asked, opening his arms wide to reveal the destruction around him. "Your city has crumbled beneath my feet. How long do you think it will take for the rest of this pitiful world to bow before me?"

"We'll never bow before you. Someone'll stop you. "

"Ah, the young girl speaks."

Raman walked over to Linzi, grabbing her roughly by the hair and yanking her head back.

"Leave her alone," Victoria spat.

"Silence. You will speak when spoken to." He turned back to Linzi. "And who among you, little girl, is strong enough to fight a god?"

His face was only inches from hers. She could smell his putrid breath. But a rebellious fire burned deep in her eyes as she stared back at him. Defiant.

"Voltage."

Raman swept away from her, his cloak billowing out behind him.

"Ha! This Jonas creature has memories of the one you call Voltage. Pathetic. My one-eyed dog defeated him with ease. I'm afraid he won't be saving you any time soon."

No, Linzi thought, as Raman's laughter filled her ears. If Voltage had been beaten, who else was left to stop this monster? Who would save them?

Raman motioned to Pulse. "Dog, take them to the museum. I will have some fun with them later. My vanguard and I will continue devouring this city."

"Yes, my master."

Pulse forced the two women off the platform. He motioned for some soldiers to follow him in the direction of the museum. He looked back over his shoulder at Raman. His single eye glared at the man before he continued walking away.

***

Night was beginning to descend as Kellen opened his eyes. At some point he must've fallen asleep. Others around him were whimpering gently in their slumber, no doubt having nightmares about Raman. Everything was so hopeless. He still didn't feel any different. Whatever Pulse had done to him, it'd switched his powers off for good.

No. After all the time he had spent not wanting the powers, he couldn't accept not having them at all. There was no way on God's Earth he was going to give up now.

Standing to his feet, he made his way over to the cage door, careful not to attract any attention from the guards. There was a large metal lock around the bars. It looked like a giant padlock. Kellen closed his eyes and took a deep breath, placing his hand around the metal loop in the lock. If he could just get some of his power then he could use the friction to melt the lock off.

Nothing.

He focused his mind harder. Still there was nothing. His frustration was beginning to grow. He took another deep breath, his head beginning to pound. He moved his hand up and down, but still couldn't feel the familiar vibration.

Suddenly, there was a metallic taste in his mouth. He opened his eyes. He watched in awe as his hand moved so fast it was just a blur. Smoke was beginning to come off the lock. Then it fell off, falling to the floor with a clang. A few of the kids stirred, rolling over on the floor. But there were no guards. It was about time he had some good luck.

He quietly swung the door of the cage open and stepped out. He had to get his uniform back before he could really let rip. There was a spare in the professor's office, but it would take a miracle to get there without being caught by any of the soldiers – the un-dead or the live ones. What he needed was a distraction.

Just as he was rounding the corner, he spotted a sight for sore eyes. He made his way over to the cage.

"Hey, Dan, wake up," he whispered, nudging his friend in the back.

Dan stirred but didn't get up. "No, Mom. The giant cookie monster ate them."

"For God's sake, Dan. Get up!"

He nudged harder, adding a little electric shock.

This time Dan shot up as if he had been stabbed by a needle. He looked around, brow furrowing in confusion. Then a huge grin spread across his chubby cheeks.

"Kellen, I knew you'd find a way to save me. I never gave up on you. Honest."

"Look," Kellen replied. "I haven't got time for a reunion. I need a distraction and you're the best person I know for the job."

"Okay, but how're you going to bust me out? Oh, are you going to make your molecules vibrate so that you can faze through the bars and then faze me out?"

"No, I'm going to break the lock. I'm not the Flash!"

Kellen did the same as before. Within seconds, the lock was off and Dan stepped out of the cage. He was free.

"What do you want me to do?" he asked. "Break some skulls?"

Kellen looked around. "Wait, where's Professor Drake?"

"I don't know. The last time I saw him, he was on that mechanical platform thingy, but they never took him with them. He must be around here somewhere."

"Okay, we'll find him afterwards. I'm going to get my spare uniform from the professor's office while you make a distraction. Now don't get excited, I can't risk you getting hurt. Just do something simple, like run around and not get caught," he gave Dan a wink. "It's not like I'm going to be long."

Before Dan could answer, his friend was gone.

He jumped up and down on the spot, screaming his head off. It was working. Other students were waking up and banging on the bars, adding to his special brand of chaos. The guards tried their best to settle everything down, but Dan managed to duck and dive around them, keeping out of their way. It felt like he was doing it for an age. His face had turned bright red, his blood pounding in his ears. If Kellen didn't hurry up, he was going to pass out, he realised. He tried to breathe, but he was running out of steam.

A black streak smashed through one of the upstairs windows and landed in the middle of the quad. Brilliant blue streaks of lightning shot into the air along with soldiers screaming for their life. Within seconds, Kellen, now dressed as Voltage, was placing the professor down next to him.

"Wait here," Voltage said to Professor Drake. "I'll be back in a second. It's time to kick this into high voltage!"

The pair of them watched as the young vigilante zigzagged around the quad, fighting his way through the soldiers, dodging bullets as he went. It was a sight to see. Voltage sent out sparks here and there, zapping them into submission. At other times, he would use his newfound acrobatic skills to roll and dive, adding his own special electro-punch to the end of the manoeuvre and knocking out anyone on the end. Within minutes, all of the students were free and the guards put in their place.

Voltage stood in front of them smiling.

"I told you it wouldn't take me long."

"Man, that was frickin' awesome," Dan said, wrapping his arms around his friend in a giant bear hug. "Kel—, I mean Voltage, I knew you could do it. You're a hero, dude."

The professor put a hand on each of their shoulders.

"It isn't over yet," he said, his voice taking on a grave tone. "The city is in chaos and the authorities are no match for Raman the Destroyer."

Voltage looked Drake dead in the eyes. "I can do this, Professor."

"Legend says that he's some kind of Egyptian god, trapped in that staff. You will need to find a way to reverse whatever process Jonas has carried out on himself. He's powerful. Probably more powerful than anything else in this world."

"I'm ready."

Professor Drake forgot himself and gave Voltage a long hug. He was so proud of the boy that was growing into a man. Dan coughed, ending the moment.

"And anyway," he said, casually putting his hands in his pocket. "It's not like you're going to be on your own this time. You'll have your trusty sidekick next to you."

Voltage looked at his friend and smiled. "I wouldn't have it any other way."

"Good luck to you both," Drake said. "I shall stay here and make sure the rest of the students are safe. The hopes of the city rest with you, Voltage. You must find a way to stop him."

Voltage clenched both of his fists. "I will, Professor."

"Godspeed."

Drake stood back as Voltage took hold of Dan's hand and shot off out of the school grounds. They were gone. He looked up at the dark sky, closing his eyes. The first raindrops began to fall as he went to help the other students.

Chapter Twenty

Voltage skidded to an abrupt halt on top of one of Zygonia City's tallest high-rise buildings. The view of the devastation was immense. Everywhere he looked buildings had toppled, men and women ran screaming in the street, trying to get out of the way of the un-dead soldiers. It was chaos. In the distance, he could see the vanguard making their way to City Hall. He would get to those, but for now, they would have to wait. There was someone else that he needed to stop first. There was a score to settle.

Dan stood behind him, almost in shock.

"A little warning next time would be nice, dude," he said, shaking.

"Sorry," Voltage replied, still staring out over the city. "It can be a little disorientating at first. You'll get used to it."

"Get used to it? You mean I have to do that again?"

"You can always stay here."

Dan looked around at his surroundings. A bemused expression passed over his face.

"Why *are* we here anyway?" he asked.

"I'm searching for Linzi and Agent Enhardt."

"So you have X-ray vision now?"

"Nope."

"Okay, now I'm really confused. How the hell are you going to find them standing up here?"

"I'll explain later. I need to concentrate."

Voltage focused his mind in to a point and then sent it out questing, searching for their individual bioelectrical signatures. It didn't take him long to find what he was looking for. They were in the museum, but they weren't alone. In the middle of the building was the strongest signature he'd ever felt, except for one time. Pulse was guarding them, no doubt waiting for him to show up. In essence, they were walking into a trap. But Voltage was ready this time. There was no way he was going to make the same mistake twice by underestimating his opponent. This time it would be him who would be victorious.

He turned back around to face his friend. "Right," he said, grabbing Dan by the shoulder and preparing to speed off. "We're heading for the museum."

"Um, did I miss the part where you actually said what the plan was?"

Voltage rolled his eyes. "Just follow my lead."

"But…"

Before Dan could finish the sentence, they were speeding off the roof. Within milliseconds, they were tucked away down some dingy alley, behind industrial dustbins, opposite the museum.

"I don't think I could ever get used to that."

Voltage didn't answer. He looked around. The fighting here had ended, leaving only devastation in its wake. His fists clenched in tandem with his jaw muscles. They'd destroyed the city. His city. Now he would destroy them.

He moved himself closer to Dan so that he could hear him.

"I need you to do what you're best at," he said, keeping his voice to a barely audible whisper.

"What's that? Looking awesome? Being suave and sophisticated?"

"This isn't a game, Dan. You see those soldiers over there?"

Dan looked around and nodded.

"Well, they have guns and they *will* use them. You need to get yourself together because I can't do this on my own."

For the first time in his life, Dan looked serious. "What do you need me to do?" he asked.

Voltage put his hand on Dan's shoulder. "I'm going to need you to create a distraction."

"Okay, I think I can do that without being shot. What're you going to be doing?"

"While you distract the guards," Voltage said, pointing to the roof. "I'll speed past and get to the top of the building and go through the skylight. There're only a few guards inside. I can take them out with ease."

"Why can't you just take these guys out?" Dan asked, looking confused. "If it's that easy, I mean?"

"If I take these guys out, there's more chance of them alerting the other grunts inside. Pulse is in there. The last thing I want is for him to know that I'm coming."

Dan looked over at the museum, unsure of whether this was a good idea or not. He looked back at his friend. Even though Kellen was behind the mask, Dan knew that his friend would go in with or without his help.

"Okay," he said, keeping his voice low. "I'll do it."

Voltage nodded. For a few moments their eyes locked together, neither one of them saying a word. For all he knew, this might be the last time that they saw each other. Anything could happen.

He shook Dan's hand.

"You've been the greatest friend a guy could ask for. It's been an honour."

"Don't you go getting all weepy on me, dude," Dan replied, trying to lighten the mood. "We've still got a year and a half of high school left. If you think you're getting out of it just because you're a hero, then think again. There's no way I'm going to sit through American history all on my own."

Voltage laughed. "Thank you."

Dan just nodded. He stood up and turned towards the museum. "This is it," he said. "Wish me luck."

Before Voltage could answer, Dan was already several steps out in the open.

"Good luck, my friend," Voltage whispered under his breath before shooting off in the opposite direction.

The rain had just begun to poor.

***

Voltage was on top of the museum roof in seconds. He peered over the edge to check that Dan was okay. What he saw made him chuckle. He was telling the guards something about a flying bunny rabbit. They just seemed to look at him in confusion. If all went according to plan, they would take him in and put him with the rest of the prisoners. Voltage wanted to stay and watch to make sure it went that way, but there was no time. For someone who could move at the speed of light, time was turning into a precious commodity. And he was sorely lacking in it.

Without making a sound, he made his way over to the skylight, all the time keeping his ears trained on what was going on out front. If he heard so much as one loud bang, he'd be down there in a flash. He could move faster than a speeding bullet.

One of the windows in the skylight was wide open. Voltage peered over the top. It was clear. It would be easy to get in. A little too easy, but it was his only option.

He lowered himself in, feet first, taking the strain of his weight on his arms as he dangled in mid-air.

I've got to get to the gym, he thought, panting. The drop was further than he realised. If he just fell, he'd either break his legs or make so much noise that it would alert any lurking soldiers. Then a smile crept across his face.

Closing his eyes, he began to swing his legs around in circles, slowly so as not to rocket straight out of the roof. After a few seconds, he picked up speed, the upward force relieving some of the tension from his arms. Within thirty seconds, small twisters were forming beneath his feet. Nearby tapestries were beginning to blow off the walls. He'd have to make his move fast or he could bring the whole building down. He opened his eyes and let go.

When he looked down, he was floating in mid-air on top of the twisters, his legs spinning like crazy. But he had no idea how to get down.

"Did you catch the game last night?" a voice said from down the hallway.

"Nah, man. The wife went in to labour. That's why I took this gig. Babies aren't cheap."

Voltage had to control his panic. The voices were heading straight for him.

He tried to slow his legs, but it had no effect. They were getting closer and closer by the second. He would be smack bang in the middle of them as soon as they rounded the corner if he didn't move fast. The twisters were dissipating, but not fast enough. If the guards saw him, his cover would be blown, putting everyone downstairs in danger. He'd have to jump.

"Congratulations, dude," the first voice said, mere feet away.

"Thanks, Mike. I really appreciate it.

Voltage jumped.

He managed to tuck himself in to a roll as he landed, sending himself flying into a broom cupboard with a loud bang. The two soldiers came rushing down the corridor.

"Did you hear that?" Mike said, pointing his gun in the direction of the broom cupboard.

"Yeah I heard it. Go take a look."

Mike inched forward, levelling his gun at the door. Beads of sweat dripped off his forehead. His breathing quickened. Heart pounded. He was beginning to regret taking this job.

He'd heard what'd happened to the last guys working with the creep downstairs.

He burst in to the broom cupboard, flashing his gun in every direction. There was nothing there. He laughed at his own fear.

"There's nothing here," he said, still checking behind some paint pots. "Probably just a cat."

His partner never answered.

Mike spun around, spotting the AK47 lying on the floor in the middle of the corridor. He inched his way out of the cupboard.

"Harley, you there?"

No answer.

He continued to walk forward, gun shaking up and down.

"Okay, Harley. This isn't funny, dude. Where the hell are you?"

"He's taking a nap."

Mike spun around, straight into Voltage's fist, sending him out for the count.

Voltage dragged the unconscious man in to the broom cupboard and shut the door. He quested out, checking that there were no more guards on this level. It was empty. He pinpointed where all of the other guards were, drawing in some reserve energy for the fight.

He took one deep breath then shot off.

One by one, he systematically took out all of the guards on each level as he went down. Pulse was on the lowest floor, guarding the prisoners himself. Voltage had succeeded in keeping his presence quiet up until now.

He zoomed in to the area containing the Egyptian display.

"Voltage!" Linzi shouted, pulling on her restraints.

"'Bout time you got here," Agent Enhardt said, a hint of derision evident in her voice. "I thought you were the fastest man alive."

Voltage looked around. Pulse wasn't here, just a generator giving off the same electrical signal. He rushed over to Victoria.

"I'm sorry," he replied, trying to untie her bonds. "I didn't mean for you to get hurt. I won't let it happen again."

"I'm okay," Victoria replied. "Go save the girl."

Voltage shot over to Linzi.

"It's okay, miss. I'll have you out of here in a—"

"Look out!"

He didn't even hear the words, just felt himself being lifted off the floor and slung against the far wall. His head cracked against the concrete, sending a crack streaking down the plaster. He landed in a heap on the floor.

"Did you really think it would be that easy?" Pulse asked, walking towards him.

Voltage spat some blood on to the floor, lifting himself up.

"You're getting sloppy, old man."

Without skipping a beat he sent out a streak of lightening in his opponent's direction. Pulse caught it with ease and threw it back. But Voltage knew it was coming and dodged it, speeding around behind the older man.

Fist after fist rained down, most of which Pulse managed to block. He threw a foot into Voltage's ribs, then an uppercut to the face with some added energy, sending the masked vigilante reeling backwards.

"I see you've improved since we last met," Pulse sneered, wiping some blood from the corner of his mouth. "I could do with a better work-out."

Voltage stared back at him, chest rising and falling. He could barely stand after the last hit. There was no way he could beat the man in hand-to-hand combat, he realised. He'd have to be smart.

He quickly looked around. "Hey," he shouted at Pulse. "Remember this?"

Without waiting for an answer, he shot a bolt of electricity straight through an exposed pipe, causing the water to explode out in to the room. In the next breath, he sent a second bolt out at the puddle forming around Pulse's feet.

The room exploded in to an electrical maelstrom, static flying all around.

But when Voltage looked up, Pulse had Linzi around the throat. He was completely unharmed.

A sadistic laugh echoed around the cavernous room. "Did you really think I'd fall for that twice? If that's the best you've got, then Zygonia City is truly doomed."

Voltage couldn't believe it. There was no beating this guy. And now he had the woman he loved at knife point. One false move and she was gone. Forever.

"Let her go, you animal," Victoria spat at him.

Pulse laughed it off. The same sick sadistic laugh.

"I wonder," he began. "If you're faster than the flick of my wrist, do you think you could stop me from slitting her throat?"

"No, I'm not that fast," Voltage smiled. "But he can."

Dan had crept up behind and smashed the butt of the gun across the back of Pulse's neck. The blow sent him and Linzi reeling forward, giving her enough time to stamp on his foot and elbow him to the jaw. It was all the opening that Voltage needed.

He flew in to Pulse, flying with him up the steep steps. They smashed through the skylight, landing in a heap on the roof.

The rain poured down on them. Voltage looked like a demon in his mask as he threw as many electro-punches as he could, causing Pulse to stagger backwards.

Voltage stopped and shot to the other end of the roof. Pulse stood there swaying, eye-patch half-hanging off.

"I'm taking you in," Voltage shouted over the din of the growing storm. "Then I'm taking your master down too."

Pulse continued to laugh in his face. "I wish you the best of luck," he said, spitting out more blood. "I never did like that pig." He launched his hand forward.

Voltage could feel the familiar pressure in his head. His assailant was rooting around in his mind. Not again, Voltage thought, panic rising in him. If he lost his powers a second time, there was no way he would be able to get them back. He wouldn't let it happen. Not again.

With all his might, he sent a massive shockwave in Pulse's direction. A huge sonic boom rang out as Pulse used his own energy to try and block it.

The explosion flung him from the roof.

As soon as Voltage had gathered his senses, he zoomed over to the ledge and peered over the side.

There was nothing. No body, no blood marks. Nothing. Pulse had disappeared.

He sent out his senses, questing for the man, trying to find any small sign that he was still out there. But still nothing.

Deep down, Voltage knew that this wouldn't be the last he saw of the man with the scar. But for now he was gone; for now Voltage had won.

Making the sign of the cross, he shot off back in the direction of his friends. Soon, he'd be having the fight of his life...

Chapter Twenty-One

As Voltage came down the stairs, he saw his friends huddled in the centre of the room, discussing the recent events. A part of him wanted to remain with them. Safe. But he knew deep down that he had a job to do. Pulse had only been the beginning. Raman was still out there wreaking havoc on the city. The world was counting on him. Voltage had no idea how he was going to defeat the monster, but he had to try; even if it meant dying in the process.

Linzi saw him standing in the archway and ran over to him. "Voltage, we thought you were dead," she said, wrapping her arms around him.

"No, I'm okay. I can't say the same for Pulse though."

Victoria came over.

"Is he dead?"

"I'm not sure," he replied. "But I do know that he's gone for now."

Victoria looked at Linzi and then back at him, giving him a wry smile. "Nice job, hero," she said.

"Thanks, Agent."

Voltage let go of Linzi and stood off to one side so that they could all see him. He was pleased that he'd finally got some acceptance from Agent Enhardt, even if it was begrudging. Maybe now they could work together without the tension hanging over them. He had a feeling he would need her before the day was over.

"The fight isn't over yet," he explained. "That monster that has taken the city is still out there and I'm the only one who can stop him. You three need to get to safety before any more soldiers arrive."

"And how do you propose we do that?" Victoria asked, folding her arms across her chest. "The whole city is crawling with soldiers, some of which aren't even alive."

Dan cleared his throat, trying to gain everyone's attention. "I can help get us back," he said, looking sheepish.

"Who the hell are you anyway?" Victoria asked.

"Yeah, why are you here, Dan?" Linzi added, looking confused. "The last time I saw you, you were trapped in a cage at the school."

"Whoa, settle down. Too many questions."

Voltage watched as the three of them chatted amongst themselves. He knew that Dan wouldn't give the game away. He also knew that his friend would be able to get them back to the school grounds safely. For the first time in years, he felt like the luckiest man in the world.

It was as if a weight had been lifted from him. He was no longer worried about sacrificing himself in order to save the day. It'd be worth it just for his friends to live.

"So, what you're saying is that you escaped and ran nearly three miles just to save us?" Linzi asked, still trying to work out how Dan had made it to the museum.

"Well, I'm the FBI agent around here, so I'll be the one to get us to safety. But first I've got to call in. Voltage, can you—" Victoria turned, noticing that he wasn't there any more. "Where the hell has he gone? I need to tap into the police radio."

Dan cleared his throat again, causing Victoria to turn back. "Will this do?" he said, passing her a mobile phone.

Victoria snatched at it as Dan went over to stand by Linzi, who was staring out of the window at the storm.

"There's something so familiar about him," she said, turning to Dan. "Do you think he'll be okay?"

"He'll be fine," Dan replied. He looked out of the window, moving far enough away for her not to hear. "You better be okay, Kellen. Or we're all screwed."

***

Voltage rushed through the storm as fast as he could. It was hard going, dodging in and out of buildings, trying to avoid any pockets of soldiers lurking around the city. Several times he had to stop to save people trapped within the rubble. They looked startled as the masked vigilante they'd all been hearing about on the news was standing over them, helping them rather than hurting them. It wasn't exactly the debut he had in mind, but it would have to do. He was becoming accustomed to not being able to do the things he wanted to.

He skidded to a halt on top of the Zygonia News Corp building, almost toppling head-over-heels as his feet slipped on the wet surface. Reaching out, he managed to grasp hold of the rail before plummeting to the street below.

A squadron walked beneath him. He held his breath. This area of town had been turned into a military zone. If he was caught now, his element of surprise would be blown away and he would have to fight his way to City Hall. Sweat began to trickle down his neck, mingling with the rain that had soaked him through. He could feel his hand slipping. A thought occurred to him. He let go of the rail.

He splashed down right in the middle of the group. "Howdy, guys," he said with a grin. "It's raining masked vigilantes out here."

Before any of them could grasp what was going on, Voltage reduced them to a pile of sleeping babies, using the rain to increase the strength of his powers.

"Night, night, boys."

He moved over to one of the soldiers that looked around the same size as him. He grabbed him by the ankles and dragged him off to a nearby alleyway. Within a flash, he was wearing the man's uniform.

Picking up the gun, he walked down the street and headed straight for City Hall. Straight for Raman the Destroyer.

***

The area around City Hall looked like Fort Knox. Groups of soldiers marched around the streets, forcing people into prisons or fighting pockets of resistance. Voltage had managed to get within spitting distance of the building, passing through the various checkpoints that had been erected along the way without any trouble. Each one made him more nervous than the last. He needed to get closer to the main building. Closer to Raman.

"Pass, please," a grizzled guard asked.

Voltage's heart stopped. He didn't have any kind of ID. The uniform that he was wearing had been enough to get him through all of the other checkpoints. He just stood there staring at the officer, not knowing what to do.

"Yeah, you," the soldier barked. "You ain't getting through without a pass."

"I, um, I…" Voltage couldn't think of anything to say. He looked at the guard and then over at the City Hall building. He was so close. "Screw it!"

He threw out his fist in the blink of an eye, catching the guard on the chin. He went out cold. It was time to move.

Spinning like a tornado, he ripped off the army uniform and replaced it with his familiar blue lightening insignia streaked outfit. That's more comfortable, he thought, as he looked around spotting soldiers charging in his direction. His cover was blown. Now it was time to fight.

He zigzagged, speeding between soldiers, fists and feet flying left and right in a blur. Several times he managed to avoid stray bullets coming from snipers on the rooftops. He sent huge balls of electricity flying in their direction, blowing the ledges clean off the roofs. He didn't have time for subtlety. He had to get the job done. And it had to be done fast.

Scores of men were charging out of City Hall, heading straight for him. He could feel the energy in his body beginning to run low. He sent his mind out as fast as he could, locking on to the nearest power source and pulling in some reserves. There was no way he could beat an entire army on his own.

A stray bullet pinged off the pavement inches from his feet. He looked up.

"Now, that's just not friendly," he said, speeding straight for the men.

He zapped and shot electricity at as many as he could. They were slowly closing in on him. He didn't want to cause them any serious harm, but if he didn't think of something fast, he'd have no choice. It was either them or him. As far as he was concerned, he was too young to die.

Suddenly, a searing pain shot through his shoulder as he was bowled off his feet. He looked down at his hand.

The black leather glove was covered in blood. He'd been shot. More men were charging towards him. He tried as hard as he could to pick himself up, but the shock was setting in. A boot landed square in his jaw, sending his vision reeling. Then another: and another. Kick after kick came raining down on him as the soldiers attacked. The corners of his vision were starting to go black. Any minute he was going to pass out.

"Everyone stand down."

Voltage knew that voice. He peered through his blood-soaked vision.

Vinnie was standing on the main boulevard shouting through a megaphone, flanked by army reserve soldiers and the brave citizens of Zygonia. A painful smile spread across his face. Dan, Victoria and Linzi were there too. The city was fighting back.

"By order of the City of Zygonia, I'm ordering you to stand down. If you do not comply, we're going to kick your ass."

The mob charged at the soldiers, heedless of their own safety. It was all the distraction Voltage needed.

He let the static charge in his body build up and then sent it out like a lightning storm. The soldiers that had been beating him flew in all directions. With a renewed vigour, he picked himself up off the floor and zapped a few more nearby soldiers with a small electrical charge. He looked around at the onslaught.

The city was winning. But for how long, he wondered. Soon Raman would realise that his forces were being pushed back, forcing him to join the fray. But not if Voltage could stop him first.

Drawing in as much energy as he possibly could, Voltage increased the vibrations in his body. His fists clenched.

Within a flash, he had disappeared inside the building.

***

Inside City Hall, it was like a morgue. Silent. Cold. It took every ounce of Voltage's strength not to shiver. It felt like something out of a post-apocalyptic horror film. Tables and chairs were thrown all over the place, smashed to pieces. Portraits were hanging from the walls, ripped and torn from their frames. Documents were strewn all across the floor making it difficult to see the marble tiles that had been scratched and ruined beyond repair. A clanking, scratching sound followed by groaning behind him made him whip around.

Several un-dead soldiers were heading straight for him, their razor-sharp blades glinting in the gloom.

"Um," Voltage uttered, "I think you guys could use a doctor."

The closest soldier swung his sword straight for Voltage's head. But they were too slow. He ducked and dived in between them, managing to zap them with balls of electricity. Each time the skeletal forms exploded into dust. Within minutes, they were no more.

"Well that was easy. These supermodels really need to eat more."

"I find you amusing," a booming voice said from around the corner. "If you don't die, maybe I'll keep you as a pet."

Raman. Voltage didn't hesitate. He sped off in the direction of the voice.

It didn't take him long to find his target. As he ground to a halt in the biggest hall, his breath caught in his throat at the sight.

Raman the Destroyer was standing there in all his glory, his crown of flames casting an eerie glow over the throngs of un-dead warriors surrounding him.

Raman laughed. "That was merely a test," he said, his voice taking on a sinister tone. "How do you think you'll fair against these?"

He stepped back, lifting his staff in to the air. A brilliant white light glowed from its tip. The un-dead attacked.

Without skipping a beat, Voltage blasted himself off the floor, somersaulting away from them. As he landed, he clapped his hands together, causing an electronic shockwave to zoom out from him in to the first line. The un-dead soldiers flew into the air, bones cracking against the walls and falling to the floor. But still they pushed on. Voltage dashed to the left, throwing balls of electricity left and right. A well-timed blade slashed against his cheek and another to his arm. The pain in his shoulder from the bullet wound seared through him. His breathing was becoming rapid. He electro-punched the skull off the nearest un-dead soldier, sending it flying in to another. There was one more wave to go.

"Is that all you've got?" he asked, still breathing heavily. "I can do this all day."

"Attack!" Raman screamed.

As the skeletal soldiers stepped forward, Voltage grinned. "Bad move, guys."

He sent a bolt of blue lightening hurtling towards a huge chandelier overhead. It came crashing down on the soldiers, crushing them to dust.

"Impressive," Raman said, a guttural laugh emanating from his throat.

"I try my best," Voltage replied. "You should see me when I really get going."

"Your arrogance is amusing. Let's see if you're still smiling after I've defeated you."

Before Voltage could quibble, a blast of heat shot him into the air, smashing him against the far wall. That's going to leave a bruise, he thought, struggling to his feet.

Raman was upon him, fists connecting cleanly with each punch. Voltage could feel the sheer heat emanating from his attacker's body. It was beginning to burn. He tried his best to fight back, but it was like attacking someone with a bug zapper; his powers were barely making a scratch.

Raman raised his staff, hoisting Voltage into the air and throwing him against another wall.

Blood dripped from his mouth, his body beaten to a pulp. Pain racked every bone and muscle. Even his uniform had burnt away in places. But he couldn't surrender. There had to be a way of levelling the playing field.

Raman stalked towards him, balls of fire circling his free hand, his staff gleaming in the other.

"You're nothing but a worm in comparison to me, a god among men." He launched Voltage into another wall. "Do you really think you can beat me?"

Voltage coughed up more blood. He felt as though he was going to cough up his lungs at any minute. No doubt something internal had been ruptured, he realised, pushing himself on to his knees. Then a thought struck him. He sent out his senses questing for any unique signals. A painful smile lit up his face.

"Y—Y—Yeah, I reckon I—I can b—beat you," he replied, struggling to get the words out. "I—I—Is it getting windy in here, or i—is it me?"

With every last ounce of strength, drawing on every electrical output he could find, he spun his arms around as fast as he could, causing huge tornados to shoot towards Raman. The so-called god was lifted clear off his feet, dropping his staff to the floor. Voltage was only going to get one chance.

In the same breath, he shot forward, grabbing the staff from the floor with his right hand and putting his left hand on Raman's flaming skull, ignoring the pain from the fire.

As it turned out, the staff wasn't magical at all. It was scientific. It was sending out an electrical signal to Raman's brain, in turn giving him all of the powers. And if it was electrical, he could shut it down. He hoped.

"What're you doing to me?" Raman screamed.

"Sending you back where you came from."

Voltage hooked on to the signal, sending electricity to both Raman and the staff. He pushed harder, trying to reverse-polarise the signal. He could feel the static in the air building. His head pounded. Raman screamed. Voltage was going to black out. The storm raged outside.

A huge streak of lightening smashed through the roof of City Hall, hitting them both. The explosion rocketed them across the hall.

Voltage looked up. He could hear some moaning. Then nothing.

***

Across the city, plumes of black smoke rose into the air, as the fire service, aided by the heavy downpour, fought back the raging fires. The brilliant bolt of lightning had been seen for miles around. At the same instant, every un-dead soldier collapsed to the floor in a heap of bones. People came milling out of hiding spaces staring at each other, unsure of what was to come next.

But there was something in the air. It was as if the city had taken a huge sigh of relief. The fight was over. And for some reason, the people of Zygonia City felt as though they owed a debt of gratitude to someone many believed didn't even exist.

Voltage's eyes flickered open. Dan was standing over him.

"Dude, you seriously had me worried there for a minute."

Voltage tried to sit up, but his head was spinning. He fell straight back down on the gurney.

"Whoa," Dan said. "It's all over. The only place you're going to be super-speeding to now is the hospital."

"But what about Raman?" Voltage asked. He had to know.

"He's gone. No body. Nothing. No one has any idea what happened."

There were so many questions running through his brain, Voltage didn't know where to begin. But there was one question burning at the back of his mind.

"Where's Linzi?"

Dan laughed.

"She's safe," he replied. "She's back at the school helping clear up. I'm fine by the way."

Voltage laughed. It hurt, but it also felt good. "Thanks, Dan. I couldn't have done it without you."

"That's because I'm just awesome."

Victoria came marching up behind them with Vinnie in tow. "Okay," she said. "Enough of the bromance. We've got to get you to the hospital."

"Yeah, you took a pretty bad beating in there," Vinnie added.

Voltage sent out his senses, questing for an electrical source. He locked on to one and pulled some electricity in. He winked at his friend. Dan smiled.

"So," Dan said, turning to the FBI agents. "When do I get a badge? I helped you know."

"What?" Victoria asked, a look of confusion furrowing her brow. "Never. Now if you'll move out of the way I can—"

The distraction had been enough. Voltage was gone.

Chapter Twenty-Two

Kellen sat perched on his usual lofty position situated above the heart of the city. The blazing sun shone high in the sky as the festivities were in full swing below him in the street. Thousands of people had gathered outside City Hall for a huge party. A parade had already gone by and now the crowd were bopping away to the sounds of Zygonia's number one band, The Black Rose, as they performed his favourite song. The crowd roared as the lead guitarist flew across the stage performing a solo. A broad smile spread across Kellen's face. Life didn't get much better than this, he thought, as the song finished and the mayor came out to give his speech.

He could hear every word. He was detailing the exploits of the man that had saved the city, if not the world, from ruin. That man was a hero to be remembered and celebrated for his bravery. The masked man of Zygonia City had proven that evil would never triumph over good, the mayor claimed. The crowd hung on every word; he could feel their excitement rising with every beat. The whole scene was awash with bio-electricity that left him tingling with anticipation.

"And that man is here today."

"This is my moment, Bernie," Kellen said to his stone friend, as he limbered up.

"Ladies and gentlemen, I give you," the mayor paused. "Voltage!"

Kellen shot off the roof in a black blur, speeding down the building and leaping onto the stage to land in a pose with his arms outstretched as if to embrace the crowd. They roared with delight; the sound of thousands of hands clapping was like thunder in his ears. He was loving every minute of it. For the first time in his life, he wasn't just the geeky science nerd. He was accepted.

"Thank you, everybody." He let the eruption of the crowd die down before continuing. "Wow, this is such an honour. I can't believe that you've all come out here just to see me. Although, I think The Black Rose performing is far more exciting than me."

Everybody laughed at his attempt at humour. It was a relief to hear the sounds of joy after the crisis they had all just come through together. Much of the city was in ruins, but still the people managed to celebrate. They were united in victory and Kellen had never been so proud in his life.

"I vow to you here today that all the time there is blood in my veins and air in my lungs, I will never let any evil befall this beautiful city. I'll protect you with everything I have. You can sleep safe knowing that Voltage is watching over you."

Again the crowd erupted into a cacophony of emotions. Some wept tears of joy, while others screamed with excitement. They held up banners with his blue lightening logo and name plastered all over them; one group of girls near the front of the stage had even started chanting his name.

He gave them a cheeky wink as he accepted the Key to the City from the mayor. He was about to dart off stage. He turned back to the microphone, which let off a slight whine due to the static field that constantly surrounded his body. "One more thing," he said. "Stay in school, kids."

Then he was gone, leaving the crowd cheering in awe. He had to get back to change out of his uniform. There was one more event he had to attend.

***

The sun had set hours ago over the horizon of the city. Tall buildings cast their long shadows over the well-kept grass as Kellen strolled across the quad. He had a smile on his lips that beamed as bright as the stars above. Not a single cloud could be seen. He had been looking forward to this all day; it would be his first proper date with Linzi and he didn't want to be late.

He could easily speed over there, but he wanted to do it all like a normal kid; that meant no powers. He had even brought her a bunch of flowers, hoping that he didn't appear to be trying too hard. Dan had assured him that she would go gaga for them and that women always loved a man in a suit. Kellen wasn't so sure he agreed. Watching a guy scratch all evening while you were trying to eat couldn't be that appealing, he mused, as he walked around the bend whistling away to himself. He would take his sweltering hot leather Voltage uniform over the itchy polyester any day.

Not five minutes away from Linzi's place, he felt a sudden vibration around his waist. He stopped dead in his tracks. Not tonight, he thought.

"Voltage, Agent Victoria Enhardt here. Do you copy?"

Kellen was adamant that he wouldn't answer. There was no way he was going to miss his date. He took a few more steps before it vibrated again.

"Voltage, come in."

He sent out his senses, feeling for the secret frequency. "I'm off duty. Get someone else to deal with it."

At first there was silence. He prayed that he wouldn't hear any more.

"You're needed over at the docks."

"But I have a date!"

"Stop whining. You have responsibilities now and you made a promise," Victoria explained over the com-link. "Heroes don't have time to date. Now get your butt over here fast."

She was gone.

Kellen stood there, his head down and his shoulders slumped. The colourful bouquet of flowers hung lifeless in his left hand. He took one look at them. If he went on his date, lives could be lost because of his own selfishness. If he didn't go, he might never get another chance.

You made a promise. You have responsibilities now.

The words rung in his ears like chimes of doom as he sped off, a black blur rocketing through the night streets. The bouquet of flowers lay heaped on the floor.

Epilogue

"You've been reckless, destroyed school property, skipped class, sneaked out after dark," the vice principal ranted, pacing up and down the room. "Need I go on? The list is endless."

Kellen and Dan just stood there behind the desk looking sheepish. They'd never seen Vice Principal Danvers so angry. She was usually calm and collected. Now she was more scary than Raman.

"Well?" she screamed.

"No, ma'am," the two boys said in unison.

Vice Principal Danvers sighed, slumping down in her chair. She brushed her long blonde hair back out of her face. She stared straight at the boys. "What am I going to do with you?"

"You could always let us—"

Kellen shot an elbow in to Dan's ribs, imploring his friend to shut up.

"You do whatever you see fit, ma'am," Kellen replied. "We're ready for any punishment you feel is suitable."

"There's more to you than meets the eye, Mr Amos," Danvers said. "I'm not sure what it is, but I can guarantee I'll find out." She stopped, opened her desk drawer and pulled out a pamphlet for each of them. "But until then, you boys are going to be spending the summer in Arizona."

"What?" Kellen said, a little louder than he had meant to. He was hoping to have spent the summer with Linzi now that Casper was out of the way. Not only that, but who would take care of the city? "I can't do that."

"You'll do exactly as I say," the vice principal replied. "It's either that or expulsion."

"Arizona will do just fine," Dan replied.

"Good. The school has just started a new partnership with another school for students to gain extra credits in certain subjects. I do believe you both study American History?"

"Yes, ma'am," Kellen replied, reluctantly.

"Excellent. Then that is what you'll be studying. That'll be all."

Great, Kellen thought. A whole summer of more studying. No Linzi, no fun. Nothing, except sweating in a classroom. There really were consequences for his actions, he realised. They didn't even know where the school was.

"Where in Arizona is the school anyway?" he asked, as they were walking out of the door.

Vice Principal Danvers smiled. "Redrock."

***

The sun was sinking low over the desert horizon, bathing the mesa in an eerie, orange hue. All was still and quiet. Miniature sandstorms were beginning to stir. In the middle, a lone building stood out of the landscape set back from the main road that ran through the White Buffalo Reservation.

It was the notorious Rattlesnake biker bar. It was a regular haunt for many of the local criminals; an escape from the prying eyes of the law. Several leather-clad men stood sentry outside the door, raucous laughter breaking the silence. No one except the regulars would dare enter.

Inside was the biggest band of cut throats that could be found in Arizona. Some were drunk and passed out, whilst others groped the local Indian girls that had come off the reservation to earn a buck or two. In one corner of the bar, a fight had broken out among four men over a pool game. It was a regular occurrence at the Rattlesnake and something Smokey, the barman, was used to dealing with. He slowly walked over to the man instigating the fight.

Smash! He bottled him across the back of the head.

The man wobbled for a few moments, then crashed to the floor in heap. Smokey turned to the remaining three men. No one else even paid attention.

"You boys know I only have one rule. No fightin' in the bar." Smokey kept his voice level and stared at each of the men in turn. A lopsided grin crossed his stubbly features. "That gives you thirty seconds to haul your mangy asses out my bar before I cut off your privates."

Each of the men looked at one another.

"Twenty seconds, boys."

He spun the broken bottle in his hand, the sharp edges reflected in his quick eyes. He knew he could take them. He was tall and gangly, but being an ex-magician and Black Ops agent had left his hands quick. Not only that, he was White Buffalo. The spirit of his ancestors would lend him strength. These lumbering idiots were no match for his speed.

"Ten... Nine... Eight..."

Realisation that Smokey could take them dawned on the bikers' faces. They grabbed their fallen comrade and made a hasty exit. A chuckle passed his lips; no one messes with Smokey.

He went back behind the bar and in to a small, shabby office. It stunk of tobacco and whiskey. Smokey dropped in to his chair and put his feet up on the table. He looked at the paper.

It announced that the Zygonia City crime rate had dropped drastically due to the heroic efforts of its new favourite son, Voltage. In an after note, it informed the reader that clean-up efforts were ongoing and that Mr Jonas was still unaccounted for.

Smokey let out a snort of derision. No such luck. Mr Jonas was not a man to be kept down for long; he remembered him well. If it hadn't been for Jonas and his lackey Pulse, Smokey would have been rich and famous as the world's most gifted illusionist. Instead, he ended up fleeing after a botched heist for Mr Jonas, who then denied all knowledge and involvement in the plot. It was all an elaborate scheme to impress the elder Mr Jonas. He was dead now, the silly old coot, and with any luck his son would be too.

The news story had been capturing everyone's attention since it had broke. A man with real power walking the streets. Smokey didn't know whether it was a good or a bad thing. Although, it would make his life easier if his own magic tricks were real, instead of the fake kind, he mused.

He began to wonder if he would ever be that powerful. One thing was for sure, he wouldn't throw it away like Jonas.

In all honesty, though, the last few years had been good to him. He was back home with his people, had a business and respect. But something in him yearned for more. If only he knew where to find it. The ringing telephone snapped him back to reality.

"Rattlesnake Bar," Smokey informed the caller.

"Is that Jessie Tsosie?"

Smokey sat stunned. He took his feet off the table and pulled himself upright. It was a name he hadn't heard in years. "Yeah, who's this?"

"That's not important." The voice was low and seductive. "I have a proposition for you."

"Who is this?" There was something about the voice that Jessie recognised. He wasn't sure if he was interested in the man's proposition, but he couldn't stop himself from wondering what he might be offering.

"Like I said, that's not important. Are you interested in hearing my offer?"

"Go ahead." There was no harm in hearing what the man had to say.

"I need you to…" he paused. "Acquire a small item from a nearby shaman of the White Buffalo Tribe. It's just a small trinket; two amulets in fact, but they are worth a lot to me. One is of an eagle and the other of a coyote. Can you get them?"

"What's in it for me?" Jessie asked. It sounded like a simple job. He could get the amulets and stiff this caller for every penny. Maybe this opportunity had been what he was waiting for. After all, he was a master trickster.

"You may go back to your original life as a magician, unhindered by the authorities. How does that sound, Mr Tsosie?" the voice enquired.

Jessie was very tempted. He missed his old life, and this guy could get it back for him. "Okay, I'll do it, but how do I contact you when it's done?"

"Good." The voice was very businesslike now. "You have two months to acquire the items and then I shall contact you. Goodbye, Mr Tsosie."

Click. The mysterious caller had put the phone down.

Jessie Tsosie, a.k.a. Smokey, sat still in his mangy office chair. The sound of drunken bikers filtered through the closed door. This was it; this was the thing that was missing. He could feel it in his bones. Jessie would steal the amulets, wait for the mystery caller to contact him again and then he would extort money from him. Yes, he would be rich. He could afford to get his old life back. His name would be up in lights once more.

He smiled a wide grin that gave him an insane look. Out here there were no costumed wackos to stop him. Everything would be perfect.